SAM CRESCENT

EVERNIGHT PUBLISHING ®

www.evernightpublishing.com

Copyright© 2022

Sam Crescent

Editor: Audrey Bobak

Cover Artist: Jay Aheer

ISBN: 978-0-3695-0508-8

SAM CRESCENT

THE FAKE ENGAGEMENT

Sam Crescent

Copyright © 2022

Chapter One

"I hate my boss." Eliza Drake yelled the words at the same time she slammed through the door of the apartment she shared with her two best friends.

"We've already got the tequila out," Juliet Caves said.

"And she made snacks." This was Mackenzie, who shoved a bacon-wrapped jalapeno into her mouth. "Damn, that's so spicy and good."

Eliza burst out laughing as she rushed toward her bedroom, throwing her jacket and bag onto the bed and moving quickly to join her two favorite people in the whole world on the sofa. Kicking off her heels, she slumped down. Juliet handed her a glass of tequila, which she knocked back, swallowing the dangerous liquid. She shouldn't drink on a work night, but since she'd been given the job as PA by Preston Boone himself, she was working every night.

"I needed that."

Mackenzie already held out a jalapeno delight. Eliza took it, biting into the rich, spicy food. The cheese, bacon, and jalapeno danced on her tongue. She closed her eyes, savoring the taste of the food.

"So good! Another, please."

She was given another. This time, she didn't play around, putting the whole thing into her mouth and biting down.

There was nothing wrong with enjoying snacks for dinner.

"Asshole boss?" Juliet asked.

"Totally." She sighed. "Well, he was ... I typed up the letter exactly how he asked me to, and clearly, he was being a giant dick because he blamed me for all these typos and how he would never say certain words." She growled. "I'm never going back to work."

"I hear you," Juliet said.

"And me," Mackenzie said.

"Was it a bad day for you girls as well?" she asked, looking at them in turn.

Mackenzie sighed. "I think my boss's son is trying to destroy the company. He's trying to handle this multimillion-dollar investment even though his father has told him not to do it. He doesn't want his company to be swallowed up in corporate. He likes to do everything old school, but his son doesn't listen." She pursed her lips. "I have a feeling we're going to fall victim to a takeover bid. The sharks are circling."

Eliza knew how much Mackenzie loved her job. The firm she worked at was just a small place, but they offered some of the best advertising rates and also held the books of some of the most lucrative companies. Their advertising reach was far and wide. She knew this as her own boss had reached out to Doug's Advertising. A simple name, and yet, they offered such high-quality work with amazing turnaround results.

If they were going for a takeover bid, she had a

feeling Boone could be one of those damn sharks.

"My boss is looking to expand his reach into plus size, only he's being advised to use a very slim model. Who wants that?" Juliet asked.

Eliza looked at Juliet. "Why don't you offer to model for it?"

Juliet was so amazingly beautiful, with long, luscious brown locks and a figure that had most men drooling. She was plus size and wore it so well. Eliza had watched her; the way she walked and moved—she screamed seductress. Juliet would make an amazing model.

Her friend wrinkled her nose. "No please, that is never happening."

"I thought you wanted to be a model?" Mackenzie asked. "Back in school, you even said that you wanted to be a role model to girls. To show the world that you didn't have to be super slim and starve yourself to grace the cover of a magazine."

"Yeah, then I got real."

Eliza threw herself at her friend, pulling her in close for a hug. What got real was Juliet's mom, tearing down her dreams in every single direction. Juliet's mom believed only thin women were beautiful and always used every piece of ammunition to destroy whatever happiness Juliet found.

Eliza hated the woman, and while they were growing up, she'd often asked Juliet around for sleepovers. At least her own mother had been supportive of her dreams.

"You're gorgeous, and your body would sell anything." Mackenzie leaned back, giving Juliet a good looking over.

"Stop doing that. Whatever it is you're doing," Juliet said.

Mackenzie winked at her. "Yep, I totally could use you."

They all burst out laughing.

This was what Eliza had needed. A day with Preston Boone was enough to put even the happiest person in the world in a downer. Of their little group, she was the one who usually saw a light in the darkest of tunnels.

When Juliet failed one of her tests through college and thought her dreams were over, shattered, Eliza wouldn't allow that. For three weeks straight, she forced Juliet to study her ass off until finally, she was more than ready.

She'd aced that test.

Positivity in life was the key.

Glancing at Mackenzie, she remembered when she first started to work for Doug's Advertising. She'd been so down. Where Eliza and Juliet had gotten work with some of the biggest companies in the city, if not the world, Mackenzie had struggled. There were very limited openings for her kind of skills as a design artist.

There had been a time Mackenzie thought she would have no choice but to return home, but that didn't happen. It may not be a big firm, but Doug's Advertising was one of the best, and Mackenzie worked as one of their designers.

They'd always wanted to move to a big city to follow their corporate dreams. This was part of their plan, to learn everything they needed to know before branching out into their own company, one that was female driven and competitive in the male market.

She handed her glass for another tequila. "I'm going to have to quit."

"No quitting," Juliet said. "Remember. That's our motto. See the bigger picture. We'll all be happy eventually."

"Yeah, there's happiness and then there's wasting your skills picking up your boss's laundry. Or better yet, finding an adequate cleaner to handle his apartment. If that's not good, maybe it's a quick trip to a jewelry store to buy something to help him deal with his one-night stand?" She shuddered. In the past three years, she'd done all of that for Preston Boone. "I don't get it. Why do women fall for him? He's an asshole."

"He's hot," Juliet said. "Come on, guys, we've seen pictures of him, and you, Eliza, get to see him up close and personal every single day."

"Exactly, I know what a toad he is."

"You know what happens when you kiss a toad?" Juliet asked.

Eliza glared at her friend. "You get toad lips, nothing else. There are no princes waiting in the wings. We all know this."

"True!" Mackenzie ate another jalapeno.

"I'm sorry. I'm not going to worry about this." She put her glass down and ran her hands over her face, trying to clear her mind of her worries. It wasn't exactly happening.

She was so tired, like all the time.

Preston was a full-on, all-the-time boss.

Even in the middle of the night. He'd called her to make notes. The first time he did that, she thought she was going crazy. She'd been working for him for two days, and he called her at three in the morning for her to make a couple of notes about what he wanted to broach at one of the meetings he had booked.

The next day, he told her to scrap the ideas because they were the ramblings of a tried man. He rarely used the notes he asked her to take first thing in the morning.

A giant asshole.

She had gotten used to it though. Beside her bed, she slept with her cell phone, coffee, a notepad, and even some migraine relievers.

A full night's sleep was rare.

"At least you made it home for girls' night," Juliet said, putting a hand on her knee.

"Yeah, but look at us, we're all tired," she said.

Juliet looked exhausted.

Mackenzie kept stifling a yawn behind her hand.

"We're fine." Mackenzie waved her hand. "It's been months since we last got wasted and just stopped caring about what our bosses, or bosses' sons, did. We need to learn to switch off, you know." She nodded. "Give me the tequila and let's turn some music on. We're still young and carefree. I'm not going to let my boss put a downer on this evening, like ever." She took the bottle from Juliet and gulped it down.

It must have been worse than Eliza thought.

For Mackenzie to drink from the bottle, it meant she wanted all her worries to disappear. They were all going to be in a bad condition tomorrow, but right at that moment, Eliza didn't care.

"You're right. We need to shake off all parts of work." She got to her feet and right there in front of her friends, who were more like sisters, she tugged open her blouse and then wriggled out of her pants. Standing in a pair of matching panties and bra, she held her hand out for the tequila.

Mackenzie handed it right to her, and she took several gulps.

Tomorrow didn't matter. She was tired of being perfect, or at least trying to, and her boss finding small insignificant details to complain about. That was all he did, and she hated him for it.

If she got the wrong coffee, he'd spend a good ten minutes telling her the importance of using the right coffee from the correct company. She had dared to buy him a bagel for lunch with full-fat cream cheese, and he'd started to complain about the damage of eating full-fat anything. Personally, to Eliza, if you were going to spend your time eating something, then eat what you loved. Don't go for low-fat. Enjoy everything in moderation. It was how she worked.

Yes, she was a fuller woman, on the heavier side, dressed in a size twenty most of her life, but that was life. She'd always been bigger. Her mother had never allowed her to be ashamed of who she was but had taught her to embrace her curves, to hold her head high, which was what she did.

Always.

Juliet turned on the music, and after taking a large gulp of tequila, Eliza handed the bottle to Juliet, throwing her hands up in the air and allowing the music to take over. She wanted to forget all about her job, about responsibilities, and to just think about letting go. About partying. About fun.

Three years she'd been working for him. It was time for her to have some private time, and if that meant dancing, drinking, and enjoying some good food with her best friends, that was exactly what she was going to do.

Mackenzie and Juliet had been in her life since kindergarten. They were the best of friends. Throughout high school, some people had called them the chubby trio, and she'd told them to go and get fucked. She'd been such a badass in school.

There was no one else she wanted to spend her life with. They'd been with her through the good times and bad.

The boyfriend who had slapped her across the

face had been in for a surprise when she'd hit him right back, but she hadn't stopped with a slap across the face. She'd hit him hard, followed by a kick to the balls, and the cops had been called. He'd demanded her arrest, but the bruising cheek had been evidence of his attack. It turned out her ex had a history of hitting and beating on women. Not this woman.

Her friends had been there for her even though he tried to make them go away, trying to push them away.

They were not just friends, but sisters. From the time they were a young age and little Peter Buttface punched Mackenzie and called her fat, they had been united. They had a pact, to be the best of friends through thick and thin.

They had a bond, and nothing, no one, could separate them. If any guy wanted to date them, he had to get through her friends first, and that was a fact.

****

Preston Boone glanced at his watch for the sixth time, surprised. His PA was late. He tapped his fingers on his desk and waited.

In six minutes, he had a meeting with a prospective client he'd been trying to acquire for nearly seven months. Mr. Aguire held a large expanse of land that also homed multiple ranches. For many years, companies like his had been trying to buy the land from him. It was the perfect place for expansion. It would create jobs and add to the local investment in the area. It also helped that Mr. Aguire held multiple land contracts Preston was interested in.

He knew to get him on his side would more than triple his own portfolio. He was looking to invest into real estate, just like his daddy did back in his hometown, but this was on a larger scale. He wanted Boone houses worldwide, which was why he was looking for the right price for Mr. Aguire.

For seven months, he wouldn't take a single phone call, and all of his letters had been sent right back to him, unopened.

He didn't know how Eliza, his PA, had arranged a meeting, but now she looked to be ruining his chances of building his dream. Of taking the Boone name to the next level rather than just being the complete owner of a small town.

Pushing those thoughts to one side, he got to his feet and looked out over the city. His building was one of the largest he'd always dreamed about. From the time he was a little kid, he told his dad he planned to have the biggest company and the most employees, and he had acquired that.

Each new goal he set out, he didn't stop until he achieved it. The business world was cutthroat, brutal, and it was where he shined.

Thinking about his business and how he handled it, he knew deep down his father would be disappointed in him. The town of Westcliffe Heights wasn't founded on buying companies, tearing them apart at a man's whims.

His father had invested heavily in the town, which was why most of the companies there had Boone in the title. They pretty much owned everything, but the people there didn't hate them. His father had never been a cruel man. He'd been a fair and generous man.

"Where are you, Eliza?" he asked. He should have known she would let him down now.

Three years she'd been working for him, and he was amazed at her track record. After his last PA quit and left him in a bind, he'd been so pissed off. She'd done it on purpose as well, messing up all of his accounts as she threw his job back in his face. He'd stepped out of his office, glanced over his employees, and pointed at Eliza, then told her she was going to be his PA.

He'd never hired a person he needed so desperately in that way before. Just thinking about it, he couldn't help but cringe.

She had deserved a lot better than a finger point, a demand to get into his office, and to start doing her job.

The following day, he'd seen how angry he was and intended to find the perfect PA. He was going to go to one of those agencies that helped to find the right person you were looking for on the job.

That never happened because when he got to work, he found the five files that had been messed up the previous day. His cabinet had been rearranged, as had his desk. Notes had been neatly stacked per order of importance, along with an amazing coffee and a smiling woman.

Now, that had been a highlight of his day.

A very happy woman to come to the office to see.

Of course, over the days that followed in the last three years, the smile became rare to see, not that he was surprised. He was a hard man to work for. Still, Eliza surprised him as she hadn't quit, which was a relief.

She made his life so much easier.

"Brother! You know it's so dull to be staring out of the windows, don't you?"

He'd been so lost in his thoughts, he hadn't seen his young sister, Trudy, coming toward his office.

He moved toward her and held her tightly for a hug.

"I have missed you so much."

"And I've missed you."

Trudy pulled back and wrinkled her nose. "I have no idea what you see in the city. It's so cold and everyone bumps into you. It's like a freaking circus down there." She walked past him, going toward the window and looking down. "Fuck me, that's so far down. Is that what you do, pretend to be a king, glaring down on your subjects?"

"Very funny. Trudy, you know I love you and enjoy your trips, but what are you doing here?"

His sister never visited him at work. It was the one place she said she couldn't stand him because it was so superficial. She liked to remember him being human, whatever that meant, but he wasn't going to argue with her.

"You know why I'm here, and you know why I know that you're avoiding the subject." She spun around, her arms folded as she looked at him. "Am I right about that?"

He glared at her. "I'm busy right now. I don't have time for this conversation."

"Of course, because tearing companies down and keeping all of their good parts is what you do now. You don't call home. You don't write."

"I make it home every single Christmas, and I send presents for birthday," he said.

"No, you stay as long as is necessary, and we all know you're miserable because of it. Westcliffe Heights is in your blood. You can come here and act the big hotshot businessman, but you're a Boone, Preston. Always have been. Always will be, and that means you've got to come home for this summer party. You know Mom and Dad have been planning this for years, and if you don't turn up, it's going to break her heart."

He ran fingers through his hair, trying to find anything that could distract his sister from this line of questioning.

"They're only interested in finding me a woman, Trudy. You know this. They want me to settle down, have a couple of kids. Get married. All of that."

"And what's wrong with that? Yes, there will be lots of eligible women. Mostly single Westcliffe Heights women, but come on, Dad is wanting to retire soon. He's nearly sixty years old. You know this is important to him. To both of them."

His parents were celebrating being together fifty years. He knew that made them ten years old, and the truth was, his parents had been boyfriend and girlfriend since they were ten. His mom got pregnant at sixteen, and that was when they got married, but they always celebrated their anniversary on the first of August. The day they finally got together and shared their first kiss. They'd been best friends before that.

Marsha and Greg Boone were an inspiration to so many. Their love for one another had shocked Westcliffe Heights. There were tales of their love, and how at the age of five, Greg, his father, had declared he would marry Marsha.

"I'm not going to marry one of their women, or their picks. I'm just not."

"You're still going to embrace the playboy life?" Trudy asked. "You know it upsets them when you play this role. It's not you. Out of all of us, you were the one who said you would find your soulmate."

"Enough already." He knew exactly what he'd said growing up, but it hadn't worked out that way.

Glancing past his sister's shoulder, he saw Eliza scrambling around her desk. She wore a pair of sunglasses and her hair, for the first time ever, was not pulled back into a bun. Compared to the last three years, she looked a mess, but seeing her like this, her lack of calm, he couldn't deny she looked … sexy.

This was bad.

So very bad.

He didn't like the way his thoughts were going.

Just then, Eliza stepped into the office, holding a takeaway cup of coffee.

"I'm so sorry I'm late," she said.

Staring at Eliza, he knew he shouldn't. Eliza was his employee, one of the best ones he ever had. This was so wrong.

"It is more than fine ... darling." He had never said anything of the sort to his employee in his life. He'd berated her, told her she did good work, but terms of endearment weren't easy to say. But this was too good of an opportunity to pass up. If he appeared to be dating someone already, his sister would report the news to his parents, and there wouldn't be any pressure to go on a date. It was stupid, irrational, and the moment he called Eliza *darling*, he knew he'd regret it.

She paused and looked at him, still wearing the sunglasses.

"Mr. Aguire is due to arrive any minute. I've got people setting up the conference room, including all of his favorite snacks and treats."

"Yes, that's good." He reached out, taking Eliza's hand and pulling her close, not too close. "I want you to meet my sister."

Eliza tensed up.

This was so wrong on so many levels. She could slap his ass with a sexual harassment lawsuit or something like that.

"Preston, what's going on?" Trudy asked.

"Trudy, I'd like you to meet my fiancée, Eliza Drake. Sweetheart, I know we wanted to keep our love a secret, but my sister is on a need-to-know basis."

"Fiancée?" Eliza and Trudy both snapped together.

Eliza turned to look at him. She pulled the glasses

from her eyes, and he saw they were a little bloodshot. Someone had too much tequila last night. He would tear into her about that later, for now, he needed her to focus on the problem at hand.

He cupped her cheek, trying his best to be earnest. "I know you wanted to keep our relationship a secret, but she's family, and I can't keep something so big from family."

She glared at him, and he was willing to give her anything if she named her price.

Eliza spun away from him, looking at his sister. "I'm so sorry. I didn't mean to be introduced this way."

"This is the first I've heard of it," Trudy said.

"You know I don't like to date employees, but our feelings wouldn't disappear."

"Is this why you hired her?" she asked.

"No, no, no, no," Eliza said. She started to laugh. "Of course not. I am good at my job. I guess it was all the late nights, you know."

He put his hands on her shoulders. "That's exactly right. It was the late nights. We were constantly working together, and one thing led to another." He didn't know why he was elaborating on this lie any further. "So, as you can see. You can tell Mom and Dad not to bother with anything else."

Trudy smiled, and he hated that look on her. It meant she was conspiring. "Oh, don't worry, I'll let them know. I take it you will be bringing Eliza with you to Westcliffe Heights? The whole family is going to want to meet the woman who has captured your heart. Do I get to see the ring?" Trudy asked.

Eliza slid her hand behind her back, and he sighed. "I had to get it resized. It was too big for Eliza's finger."

"Right, of course. This totally sounds legit."

"Trudy, I'm needed for my first meeting. Can we take a raincheck on this conversation and continue it later?"

"Yes. I won't get in the way of work, but I cannot wait to get to know the woman my brother has fallen for."

Trudy pulled Eliza into a tight hug.

"We are going to be such good friends."

Chapter Two

What the hell just happened?

Eliza took the necessary notes, but the meeting with Mr. Aguire was turning into a complete disaster. She offered reassuring smiles and tried to help the meeting run smoothly, but inside, she was reeling.

Fiancée?

What the hell had just happened? She had no idea what was going on. Was it some kind of joke? Was Preston pissed off because she was late? It made no sense for him to call her his fiancée.

Clearly the tequila had messed with her head.

The meeting came to an abrupt close when Mr. Aguire said he'd heard enough and walked out of the conference room.

This wasn't good.

She'd never had a meeting go this appallingly. Not in the last three years.

Eliza turned to look at Preston, but he'd also left the room. She was the only one inside, and she was more than happy to collapse into the nearest chair and just take stock of everything that had happened that morning.

First, her alarm didn't go off.

Juliet was always up two hours before everyone else, so there was no reason to expect a wake-up call from her. It was Mackenzie, who had a half day, who finally woke her up at eight-thirty, giving her thirty minutes to change, grab coffee, breakfast, and get to work. It didn't work.

Ten minutes after waking up, she'd still been throwing her guts up.

Real smooth.

She leaned forward, putting her elbows on the table. Then she found her favorite pantsuit, her lucky one, was for some odd reason shrunken, or she'd put on a few inches in weight, which was more or less the reason it didn't fit.

"So stupid."

From then, everything had just taken a turn for the worst.

Preston's favorite coffee shop was closed, meaning she had to go to the place he hated, and of course, they didn't have his favorite creamer either. Another bad point against her.

Next, as if that wasn't bad enough, breakfast, the bakery was also shut for a refurbishment. Not that she could stand food. Her stomach had been turning all morning. Tequila was the worst, and she was suffering for it.

The meeting had been a complete disaster. Preston loved to impress his clients or at least his potential clients with the bakery he used. Everything was substandard, she knew that, and had apologized for it.

Preston was going to fire her ass, and it was all her own fault. Technically, it was all his fault. Yes, that was what it was. His fault.

Eliza groaned.

Nothing had gone right today.

You're a fiancée.

Jerking up from her pity party of a bad day, she got to her feet and immediately went storming toward his office. They didn't have time to discuss his little outburst at his sister, but she wasn't done.

He was on the phone when she entered his office, which annoyed her, because she hadn't been at her desk to direct the call.

"That will be all for now, Eliza," he said.

She tapped her fingers against her thigh.

It would be so easy to walk out, to not give him a

second or third glance, but something told her to stick around.

He shook his hand at her as if to tell her to get out.

Not happening.

She walked up to his desk, took the phone out of his hand, and pressed it to her ear.

"I'm so sorry, Mr. Boone will have to call you back." She slammed the phone into the cradle and looked at him.

"I do not know who you think you are, Miss Drake, but after this morning's performance, I'm not amused."

"Oh, really, you're not amused? Well, guess what, Mr. Boone, I could go right down to HR and file a complaint about you with regards to sexual harassment along with what happened this morning. So, why don't we both agree that today is not a very good day, and you tell me what this morning was all about?" she asked. "Your sister isn't some woman you want to get rid of, she's family."

Preston put the tips of his fingers together and leaned back.

"Well, seeing as you hung up on my parents, then I guess I should inform you that your presence for next Friday will be required, as my fiancée, back at my hometown of Westcliffe Heights."

Eliza opened her mouth, closed it, and opened it again.

"You're speechless."

She heard movement outside the office and quickly went to the door, closing it so they could have some privacy. Whirling around, she saw he hadn't moved.

"I'm not speechless, but there is no way I'm

going to your hometown."

"Not only will you go to my hometown, but you will also play the role of my fiancée, is that clear?" he asked.

She knew he could be a hardass. He hadn't risen in the ranks, producing one of the best companies in the world, by being soft. Preston Boone was used to getting what he wanted.

"No."

"You're telling me no?"

"Pretending to be your girlfriend—"

"Fiancée."

"Fine. Fiancée isn't part of my job description."

"After this morning's performance, I have plenty of grounds to fire you."

She burst out laughing. "You're kidding, right?"

"I don't make jokes about such matters."

"Mr. Boone, you and I both know I'm the best and longest-serving PA you've ever had. You want to fire me and go that route, fine. One bad day out of the three years I've served as your PA isn't bad. Not to mention all the years I worked before that." She'd started in his company as a temp straight out of college. His company offered the chance to a select few students. She applied, got the job, and worked up the ranks.

Getting the job as PA at twenty-six had been a huge achievement, but she'd always been a firm believer in hard work, and this time it had paid off.

"You need this job."

"And you need me," she said. The truth was, with her skills and how closely she'd been working with Preston Boone, there would be plenty of job opportunities available to her if she wanted them.

There was a reason she was with Boone though. He was the best of the best at what he did.

The only way to succeed in this world was to learn from the best, and that was exactly what she was doing.

Lips pursed, they glared at one another.

She had learned the hard way not to submit to Preston. He would walk all over her if he could. He was a hard boss to please.

Preston sat back. She took a seat in front of his desk.

As they stared at one another, Eliza knew deep in her heart she didn't want to lose this job. It had so many amazing benefits. It came with a great deal of faults, like the three-in-the-morning calls, and not much room for a social life, but who needed one? That was what social media was for.

"I don't know when I gave you the idea that we were friends, Eliza."

"You've never given me that idea, Mr. Boone, but seeing as today I was introduced to your sister as your fiancée, I think I have a right to know what's going on."

He sighed. "Fine. For the next month, I need you to play the part of my fiancée. You will pretend to be in love with me."

At this, she couldn't help but snort at.

"And you will be convincing."

"And if I don't?"

"Then I will let you go with a severance package."

She wasn't ready to lose this job. "And if I agree to it and play my part perfectly?"

"Then I will double your salary along with the guarantee that your job will never be in jeopardy. I will have it contracted in writing that the only way you can be let go will be at your own decision."

This man was playing hardball.

A job guarantee.

"But I would be allowed to leave at any moment I saw fit?"

"Yes."

She nibbled on her lip, thinking about this newfound offer.

"Of course, it would also require you to revoke your threat of sexual harassment. Also, whatever happens on this trip will stay on this trip."

"Kind of like in Vegas?" she asked.

"Only it will be in Westcliffe Heights."

She sat back, a little in shock. "This means that much to you?"

"No, it means a lot to my parents."

"And you've got no problems lying to them about your personal life?"

"My parents want me to settle down, as most parents do with their children. I have no desire to marry."

No, she didn't for a second believe he did. This man was a playboy through and through. He had so many notches on his bedpost, she was surprised it fit into one room. She had lost count of the number of times she'd purchased jewelry on his behalf, or flowers. Rarely did the jewelry come back, but she'd experienced flowers thrown in her face. Some women were so rude. It wasn't like she wanted to be the bad guy. It was the role Preston gave her.

"You're not worried about any potential boyfriend I might have?"

"On your file, it states you are single, not in a relationship."

"I might not have updated that file."

"Eliza, I need your answer."

"Can I take time to think about it?" she asked.

He sat back. "Fine. Take the rest of the day off, and then I will have your answer first thing tomorrow."

She got to her feet, nodded her head, then turned to leave. After she went to her desk, she grabbed her jacket and bag and rushed toward the elevator. Pressing the button for the main floor, she waited for the elevator to arrive.

Standing inside the metal cage with a whole load of Boone employees didn't exactly calm her soul.

She was … nervous. Her stomach did flips, like tiny butterflies had given birth inside her and were doing the mad flutters.

Eliza said her goodbyes to the reception staff and immediately left the building, going straight to a burger stand.

She was either going to throw up or finally settle her stomach, but right now, she was tired of feeling sick.

With a fully loaded burger, she walked, heading to where Juliet worked, which was a thirty-minute walk.

The heat was building, and she removed her jacket, stuffing it into her bag. She finished the burger before she made it to Juliet's office, and shoved the wrapper in a nearby trash bin as she did.

Entering Juliet's office, she waved to Kelly, who worked on the main reception. The young woman was a wannabe model. She felt the best way to get to her dream was to work for a company that dealt with and specialized in them.

Eliza made her way up to the top floor where she found Juliet seated behind a desk, typing away at a computer. No sign of her boss, nor anyone else.

"What's going on?" Eliza asked.

Juliet looked up, and Eliza felt immediate anger when she caught sight of the tears in her friend's eyes.

"Eliza, I didn't know you were stopping by."

"Forget about me. What the fuck is going on?" she asked, immediately going to her best friend's side.

"Oh, it's nothing. You know me. I'm behind on my work again."

She looked around the office and shook her head. "No. This is not you behind on your work. This is your asshole boss treating you like crap again." She pulled Juliet into her arms. If it wasn't this woman's mother, it was some asshole around her making her feel less than what she was.

Eliza was getting tired of people hurting Juliet. She wouldn't stand for it.

"It's fine. Really."

"No, it's not. I don't know what happened, but you've got to learn to stand up for yourself. Don't let them walk all over you."

Juliet sniffled. "I know. So, enough about me and my drama. Tell me what's going on with you."

"No, I will tell you more when we get to Mackenzie. She's already got our favorite table. I have so much to tell you about."

****

"I'm not crazy, am I?" Preston asked his friends.

Adam and Natasha both looked at each other before turning their gaze toward him. They had been his friends since college. They met while going to some activist event about female rights, or something like that. He couldn't remember for certain. All he did know was that they ended up at a bar, ranting and talking about putting the world to rights, and were somewhat inseparable since. Where he'd stayed a playboy, his friends had found themselves in love with one another, and he'd been best man at their wedding. The ceremony had been so amazing. Other than his parents, he'd never seen a couple so deeply in love.

He wasn't jealous of them though.

Love came to those who wanted it.

The women he knew were only after money or a way of furthering their career, and right now, he was at the top of his game. He didn't have any room in his life for distractions of any kind.

Not in the female form.

Not in any form.

He was happy with having women who were of an equal mind. They just wanted sex.

"You're talking about asking your PA to play the role of your fake fiancée?" Natasha asked.

"No, of course, that's not crazy. I mean, who would think asking anyone to be fake is crazy?"

"Both of you are mocking me," he said.

His friends burst out laughing.

"I'm sorry, man," Adam said. "But do you hear yourself?"

"I hear myself perfectly. You don't know what it's like," he said.

"I've met Eliza," Natasha said. "She's not your usual kind of woman."

"What the hell is that supposed to mean?" he asked.

"First of all, she works for you. She's got a brain between her ears. She's not a model, nor an actress." Natasha held her fingers up. "Do you need me to keep going?"

"Come on, man, since when did this happen?" he asked. "She's your PA. Do you think you're going to make this work?"

He sipped at his water.

It was rare for Adam and Natasha to have any time for lunch, but they'd called him up out of the blue. He had no choice but to cancel the remainder of his meetings himself because he'd sent Eliza off for the day, and now he sat with the two people who made sense in his world.

"I need to have a date, otherwise, it will be an endless supply of women back at home, and believe me, I do not want to be home while they parade them in front of me. If I wanted to marry any of them, I wouldn't have left." He groaned. "My life sucks."

Again, his friends laughed.

"And you think of employing your PA to do it?" Adam asked.

"Sweetheart, you do know how this goes, right?" Natasha said. "They make movies about this kind of thing. You and Eliza close together, playing the role of fiancés."

He shook his head. "Not going to happen. I will not fall in love with Eliza. She's … she's a good PA, but she's not my type."

Natasha looked at Adam. "She is so your type, Preston."

He frowned. "Are you kidding me right now? You just said yourself she isn't my type."

"Yeah, but then I started to think about it. She's not your type because she's totally your type."

"How did you marry this woman?" he asked, looking at Adam.

Adam cupped Natasha's cheek. "With ease, mate. I realized I didn't want to be without her. She is my soulmate. My very reason for existing."

"And I'm going to throw up," he said.

Natasha laughed. "She's blonde and beautiful. You and I both know Eliza is exactly what you want. She has the curves, and I've seen you smile a great deal when she's around. She makes your life easier. You know it. It's why women don't make you feel like settling down, but Eliza is different. She's the person that makes you think about getting married, falling in love, having kids, settling down, and turning into your parents."

"I hate you guys, and I hate my sister. My life is perfectly organized, and it doesn't need anyone else or anything else."

Again, his friends just laughed.

They were still laughing as the maître d' brought over their meal. It was such a good place to eat. He'd read the reviews on this place, and seeing as he was a carb lover himself, he pretty much ate here every single night.

At the sound of musical laughter, he glanced toward it, shocked to find Eliza Drake sitting at a small table with two other women. One brown haired, the other a redhead, but his gaze was drawn to the blonde.

Her hair cascaded around her. Normally, she kept those locks tied back in a firm bun, but today, it was flowing freely all around her shoulders. He wasn't going to deny that he felt the need to run his fingers through the long length, which was crazy.

He had never had any feelings toward his PA, ever.

Sure, he'd noticed she was beautiful, and a few times he'd caught himself staring at the curves of her ass and admiring the way her body looked in some of the suits she wore. He couldn't pinpoint which designer she used, but they were always amazing and fit her body so well.

When he took her with him on business trips and even to conferences, men admired her, but Eliza never showed any interest. It was like she was oblivious to the looks she got.

"Excuse me," he said.

He put his fork down, got to his feet, and walked

across the restaurant. One of her friends must have alerted her to his presence because she suddenly turned and looked directly at him.

She got to her feet as he approached.

"Eliza," he said.

"Mr. Boone."

"I hope you're enjoying your lunch."

"I am, thank you," she said. "Er, this is Juliet and Mackenzie. They're my friends and roommates."

He held his hand out and each woman shook his hand, offering him a smile. "Mackenzie, I've seen you before," he said.

"I work at Doug's Advertising. I've been on a couple of your projects."

"That's right." He'd heard the bad news about Doug's potential buyout. He didn't say anything now as he didn't know the workings within the company. When he heard of the takeover offer and the bid, he'd been tempted to step forward, but at the time, he'd been focused on Aguire and had no room for an advertising agency among his investments. He didn't like to go after companies unless he had an idea or a plan on how to work them. "I'm here with Adam and Natasha," he said, looking at Eliza.

"Actually," Eliza said. "Can we step out a moment? I'd like to talk to you."

He nodded. Glancing back to his own table, he held his hand up, mouthing that he was taking five minutes.

Following Eliza outside toward the small restaurant garden, he noticed there was no one at the tables. The summer heat was normally a welcome to many, but today, they chased the cool air-conditioning inside the restaurant.

"I had no idea you were eating here," she said.

"I'm aware."

"Look, I … I'm sorry about this morning. I was unprofessional, and between the tequila last night and the whole fiancée business, it threw me. I got a call from Mr. Aguire just before we entered."

"Oh, you did?"

"Yes. He wasn't wowed by your presentation, nor was he happy with your … reputation."

"My reputation?"

"Mr. Aguire is a family man, Mr. Boone. He doesn't like how your playboy lifestyle will reflect on the purchase of his land. He feels a family man is more stable to make better and more lasting decisions," she said.

He put his hands on his hips, annoyance gripping him. It wasn't the first time his playboy lifestyle had gotten in the way of business. He never allowed it to impact his life before, and he wasn't going to let it compromise his plans now.

"So, after everything you did this morning, and I figured with your sister already knowing, and well, I'm now rambling, but I sort of told Mr. Aguire that you were engaged. That you have changed your ways and you're not some playboy. You're a man to be trusted," she said.

This made him pause. He watched her take a deep breath.

"Pardon me?"

She groaned. "I will … I'm sorry about today, and I will go to your hometown for the next month and play the role of your fake fiancée. It's the least that I can do. Mr. Aguire will be more than willing to meet you at Westcliffe Heights, to see another side of you. The side that no one gets to see." She pulled out a piece of paper and handed it to him. "I've made all the necessary arrangements, including booking a hotel suite for him, and arranging a conference room for that day."

"This will require you to play my fiancée for months after our deal," he said.

"My job will be secured with you. I will only need to play the role for as long as Mr. Aguire waits to make the sale. Once everything has gone through, we can play break up and go about our lives until then," she said.

Preston stared into her blue eyes. She looked … nervous. Her hands kept clenching and unclenching at her sides.

"Then I guess we have a deal," he said.

"I guess we do."

He held his hand out for her to shake. She placed hers inside his, and they shook. Something hit him hard and fast as her hand touched his. He didn't know what it was, but it caused them both to pull away.

"My friends are waiting for me," she said. "Next Friday, Mr. Boone."

"Next Friday, Eliza."

She nodded at him and brushed past.

He watched her go back to her table, sitting gracefully in her seat and talking to her friends.

His hand … tingled.

What was that?

He ignored it and made his way toward his table to find Natasha and Adam still enjoying their meal.

"Well, did you get what you were looking for?" Natasha asked.

He stared at his friends with a frown. "Eliza has agreed to be my fiancée."

"First part of your plan is done then," Adam said. "Now you have to convince your parents you're both in love."

He turned to Adam. "What?"

"You're not taking your PA to your hometown,

Preston. You're taking your fiancée. Fake, or otherwise, you're going to have to start thinking about her as a loved one," Adam said.

"I'll handle it."

"I've got a hundred bucks that says he falls for her," Natasha said.

"Do not bet on my love life. You're going to lose," he said.

Adam shook his wife's hand. "I will take that bet."

"Well, I will add to it and tell you that it will never happen. In fact, once all arrangements end, I will guarantee Eliza will leave my company for good."

Natasha smiled. "Fine. How about this, if we win and you fall hard for this woman, you have to take care of our kids for four date nights."

"And if I win?" he asked.

"We'll get off your case about settling down." Natasha knew how to bargain.

"Deal." He shook hands, knowing it was the easiest deal he'd ever made.

Chapter Three

"I'm crazy. There's no way I can do this," Eliza said.

"You agreed to it the moment you told your Aguire dude that you were engaged to him," Juliet said.

"We heard the words coming straight out of your mouth," Mackenzie said.

"I thought you guys were supposed to be on my side."

"We are on your side. We're agreeing with you that this is crazy and totally not like you. I cannot wait to see the sparks fly," Juliet said, laughing.

She loved her friends dearly, but this, it was … it wasn't funny.

Eliza sat slumped on the sofa. The food she'd eaten lay heavy in her stomach, but she doubted any food she ate would settle her nerves at the moment. She'd agreed to be her boss's fiancée. This wasn't funny, not even mildly entertaining.

The days she spent with him were already long enough. Adding a fake relationship into the mix wasn't going to be doing her any favors.

"I can't," she said. "I cannot do this."

"You already agreed," Juliet said.

Mackenzie sighed. "I can see it now. The sweet touches. The knowing glances. The kissing."

"The kissing?" Eliza jerked up. "Who said anything about kissing?"

"It's going to come up, Eliza," Juliet said.

"Couples, engaged couples, kiss." This was from Mackenzie, who looked way too amused.

She shook her head. "No. I'm not doing it. I'm going to have to cancel. I'm going to have to quit my job. Cancel everything. Probably run away as well."

Her friends chuckled.

"Don't. Please, guys, stop. I feel sick." She got to her feet and started to pace. With a hand on her stomach, she tried to settle her nerves, but that wasn't doing her any good. She felt like she was going to throw up, and she probably was.

"Stop stressing about it. You're making it worse than it needs to be," Juliet said.

"How am I making this worse?" Eliza asked. "We haven't talked anything through. Next Friday, I go with him and play fake fiancée. I didn't think of kissing and touching. I figured I would be PA where I called him Preston rather than Mr. Boone."

"I thought he told you to call him that years ago," Mackenzie said.

"He did, but I always freeze up and he's always Mr. Boone to me."

"You're going to have to get out of that," Juliet said. "No one is going to want you calling your fiancé Mr. Boone."

"This sucks." She collapsed back onto the sofa.

Juliet climbed across to her and snuggled up against her side. "You know, what you could do is go and find him and you guys come up with these conditions."

"Conditions?"

"Terms. Where you both agree how far this contract between the two of you will go. You can talk about kissing. Hugging. Cuddles. All of those kinds of things," Juliet said.

"It won't be that bad," Mackenzie said. "The movies make it look fun."

"I think I'm getting an ulcer. There's nothing fun about this."

"You're seeing it all wrong is all," Juliet said.

"Go and see him," Mackenzie said. "We know how you like to plan everything. I don't know why you think this won't be any different. I bet you already have pros and cons to this, as well as a whole list of suitable outfits, not to mention potential jokes. Will you do your research on the family?"

"I don't find you funny," she said.

"She's done her research," Juliet said, agreeing with their friend.

Eliza groaned. She had done her research. After lunch, while her friends went back to work, she'd gone back to their apartment and sat down with her laptop, with Preston Boone being the main search in her search engine. There wasn't a whole lot to go on. He liked to keep his private life exactly that—private.

There were always rumors and local gossip, but nothing of any truth.

She knew for a fact the pregnancy story was fake. The model who had been the main subject of the story had stopped by Preston's office where they had resolved the news together. It had required an hour-long phone call with someone in the media, a couple of news stories she had to write and Preston vetted, and the story had been removed after a whole bunch of apologies.

Preston Boone knew how to get what he wanted.

"You know what, you're both right. I'm sitting here panicking over nothing. I should just go over there and have it out with him. Tell him what my terms and conditions are, like any self-respecting fake fiancée."

"Yeah, you go over there and tell him how it's going to be," Juliet said.

Eliza grabbed her jacket and bag, giving her friends a wave. They wished her good luck.

She got in her car and on the road, heading toward Preston's apartment. It was a forty-minute drive from where she lived. The closer she got, the higher her nerves rose. This wasn't good.

The last person she wanted to see was her boss.

Still, rules had to be arranged. They were what made her life organized.

She liked rules.

After parking her car in the spare space, she climbed out. Preston had purchased a slot for her at his apartment building because he'd been annoyed at her for being late for a meeting because of no parking.

He'd been sick, but he refused to not work just because of a little flu. He'd looked like death, but she wasn't about to tell the boss what he could and couldn't do. With his determination to work, he'd given her the same flu. She had no choice but to take a week off work. Fortunately, Preston had been more than guilty. He bought her soup and she got deliveries of it every day until she returned to work in way of an apology.

The little acts of kindness like that were what kept her working for him. He wasn't a total monster.

Once she'd keyed in the code to let her in the building, she took the elevator all the way up to his room. She had no idea what his deal was with heights. She couldn't stand them. When he stood at his office window while she was in the room, it always made her feel a little sick, and her hands would grow clammy.

One wrong move, and she imagined him falling straight through the glass. Her imagination was wild. Her mother had once told her she needed to get her head in the game and not in the clouds. She rather liked being in the clouds though. Real life tended to suck.

She arrived outside Preston's penthouse suite and knocked. It was a little after ten. She should be at home, enjoying the last few hours of her life before heading to work, but instead, she was here to visit her boss.

This sucked.

If her parents ever found out she was engaged, even if it was fake, they were doomed. Wedding plans would start happening the moment her mother heard about it. They had to keep this engagement as quiet as possible, for as long as possible.

Preston opened the door, and to her surprise, he wore a pair of sweatpants and no shirt. Perspiration covered his body, and he had a towel draped across the back of his neck.

"Eliza," he said.

"Mr. Boone."

"Please, call me Preston."

She nodded but pressed her lips together. It was so silly for her not to call him Preston. She didn't even have a good reason not to call him it.

"I wanted to … I think we should talk about … our engagement. I have a few conditions and rules."

He stepped back.

There was no sign of laughter, and for that, she was thankful. She didn't think she could handle him laughing at her, not at a time like this.

Nothing had changed in his apartment; it was still white walls and black furniture. The cliché playboy penthouse suite. There was nothing of any personal effect. No paintings. No pictures. Anyone coming into this penthouse would believe this man had no family, no friends.

She knew differently.

With his lack of personal touch, she had to wonder if his parents had been good and kind.

She pushed those useless thoughts to the back of her mind. Clearly, his parents were good, otherwise, he wouldn't be trying to trick them with this fake-fiancée stuff.

"Did I catch you at a bad time?" she asked.

"No. I finished my workout. I'm enjoying my cool down. Can I interest you in some water?"

"Sure. A water would be great." Anything to prolong this torture and lengthen out her nerves.

She followed him into his kitchen, and again, it screamed bachelor. It was so neat.

Back at her own place, they had a clean apartment, but they also lived.

The kitchen counters back at her place had a mixer, blender, and food processor. When Juliet went on a baking binge, she went at it hard. Their cupboards were stocked with all kinds of baking and cooking ingredients. Different chocolate chips and spices. Juliet liked variety, and she was one hell of a good cook. None of them had any complaints about her cooking.

Eliza cooked well herself, but not on the same scale as Juliet.

Mackenzie was banned from the kitchen. That girl couldn't even cook toast, she was that bad at it. The one time they had let her cook, they had ended up with food poisoning.

"Water or a coffee?" Preston asked.

"A water is fine."

He opened his fridge, and again, everything was neat. Her fridge looked like a bomb had gone off, and she wasn't embarrassed by that either.

She lived in her place, whereas it looked like Preston simply existed. It was rather sad.

He unscrewed the lid of his water and took several large gulps. She couldn't help but watch him. All the while, she sipped at her water. He finished the bottle, turned toward his cupboard, and put the bottle in recycling, and the cap into the trash.

"These rules," he said. "What are they?"

"Well, first, I think we kind of need to create a backstory, don't you?" she asked.

"Nope. You work for me. We're together for long hours. I think it tells itself."

"Okay, fine. Well, I don't want us to have any kind of story. We don't need anything that will trip us up. We stick to facts. I work for you. The closeness and stuff like that."

She pulled out her notebook from her bag, where she'd written down some of their potential questions.

"What made you fall for me?" she asked.

"These are not rules."

"Your family is going to have questions. We're going to need to come up with the good details so our stories are straight."

"Look, Eliza, you are overthinking all of this. We're going to see my parents, not be interviewed by the FBI. We're not aliens."

She rolled her eyes. "That is easier for you to say, but I want to cover all of my bases, and you're making this very difficult for me."

"Our engagement is new, and we're working our way through everything else. Move on. What else do you have a problem with?" he asked.

"Okay, fine. Touching. I will accept a touch on the hand, and maybe a couple of hair tucks behind my ear, but nothing else. You do not need to grab my ass, and we don't need to full-on hug. I will stand close to your side, and you can put your hand on my hip. Nothing else."

"Wow, okay. You do realize we've got to be human here and not robots?" he asked.

"Duh, yeah. Of course, I know that."

****

Preston expected her to be done with the touching

limits, but nope. He should have known Eliza wasn't going to be easily fooled. She drew a diagram of the female form, complete with breasts and a vagina. Where she marked on each part of her that was acceptable.

"I hope you understand I'm not going to be able to remember all of this."

"Yes, you will. I've seen how you are in the office. This is a piece of cake compared to all of that. Believe me, you can handle anything."

It was strange for him to feel a little more confident with her feelings about him. There was no doubt at all, no hesitation. She knew he'd be able to remember.

"Okay, so we've handled touching. Now let's get down to the kissing," she said, pushing some of her blonde hair out of the way. "No tongue. That is a strict policy for me."

"No tongue?"

"You got it."

He frowned. "But what if certain functions require tongue?"

She chuckled. "Mr. Boone, what kind of circumstances could possibly require tongue? There are none that come to mind."

He sighed. "This has got to be believable in front of my parents. They've been in love with each other since the time they were ten. They're not going to believe a peck on the cheek constitutes a marriage proposal."

Eliza pressed her lips together as she stared down at her notebook. "Fine. Fine. Of course. Still, no tongue. We can kiss and make it look real to your family. That's more than fine."

"What about my hands at this point? Will they be allowed to sink into your hair?"

"Absolutely not. You will keep them on my waist

at all times."

"A pity." He gritted his teeth together and sipped at his bottle of water.

"What is that supposed to mean exactly?" she asked.

"Nothing. Nothing at all." He wasn't about to tell her that her hair looked so soft and silky, he'd thought about running his fingers through to see if it was exactly that. Nope, he kept those sweet thoughts to himself.

They were already crossing lines of what was appropriate.

"We're never having sex," Eliza said.

"What? I wasn't thinking about sex."

She looked up from her notepad. "I know you weren't. I'm talking about this agreement we've got in place. We're not having sex, so that means separate bedrooms. We'll be staying in a hotel? If you give me those details, I can make the necessary arrangements."

"No hotel."

"Then where are we staying? Do you have another penthouse apartment back in your hometown?" she asked.

"No, I don't. We'll be staying at my parents' place."

"Won't that be a little cramped?"

He laughed, he couldn't help it. "No, it won't be cramped. You'll be in complete luxury."

"I don't care about that. I'm thinking about the sleeping arrangements."

"I'll talk to my parents about organizing a second bedroom for you," he said.

"Oh, you will?"

"Yes." What he wasn't about to tell her was that he couldn't guarantee they'd agree to it. His parents liked to think they were forward thinkers. Ahead of the game in bringing true love together. They judged everyone on their standards, and they were rarely separated as he grew up.

"Is that all?" he asked. "Do you want me to chain my hands to my sides? Not talk to you?"

She looked at her notepad. "Actually, I've still got to cover the correct dress code, pet names, and acceptable fondness."

"Acceptable fondness? What the hell? Look, I can call you darling or sweetheart. You're overthinking this way too much."

She laughed. "Are you really my boss right now?"

"What is that supposed to mean?" He didn't get this woman.

"It means we're about to pull off a giant con right now. You and me, pretending to be engaged to your parents, who have known you for forty years, am I correct in assuming this?"

He didn't justify her question with an answer.

"Exactly. I think we should cover all of our necessary basics first. This is a detailed list of what came off the top of my head, Mr. Boone. Nothing more. Nothing less."

"If you're going to be engaged to me, I think it's only fair you call me Preston."

"Yes, of course. That's right." She stopped, licking her full lips. "Preston. There, see? That wasn't so hard."

"From now until this ruse ends, that's all you call me. Preston. No more Mr. Boone."

"Fine. Fine. I can do that. It'll be easy. A piece of cake."

He happened to notice a flush building from her chest up to her face.

She scanned her piece of paper and got to the bottom with a wrinkled nose. "We've got to learn about each other. Get everything in order."

"Eliza, you're overthinking this."

"Am I? I mean, think about it. They're going to ask questions and I only just learned you have a sister."

He wasn't about to tell her he had three brothers as well. To some, his life might be a tad overwhelming.

"Look, I think the best thing for all of us is for you to forget about your list. Realize I can be a decent human being and treat you with respect, and we'll get through this."

She nibbled on her lip. When did they start looking so red and so plump? He must be losing his mind.

"You're right. Of course. You're totally right." She closed her notebook. "We've got this. I will see you at work tomorrow, Mr. Boone. I mean, Preston. I was totally going to say Preston." She smiled. "We've got this."

He didn't think they did get it, but he walked with her across his apartment building toward his front door.

She held out her hand. "See you tomorrow."

He opened the door for her and watched her leave.

With Eliza out of his apartment, he could finally think. It was about time. Stretching his arms above his head, he'd already started to cool down from his workout. His PA's nerves had interrupted his precious meditation time.

Preston headed toward the shower, putting his clothes into the laundry basket. He had a cleaner who came to his apartment three times a week and completed all of their chores in the apartment: cleaning, keeping the place immaculate, and even doing his laundry. He paid her handsomely for it as she'd taken one of the jobs right off his hands.

He never had to think about his laundry. Before he went away to college, his mother had taken him through her program of laundry cleaning. He'd been determined to get away from Westcliffe Heights, and because of that, she'd forced him to do an entire summer of laundry. From gathering it out of his brothers' and sister's rooms, to actually washing their clothes, separating out the dark colors, as well as the delicates and lingerie. He'd been shown how to hang it out on a washing line, and also how to treat clothes in a dryer. His mother had been thorough and also provided a written exam.

It had been humiliating, as his brothers hadn't wanted to leave the nest. They'd gone to college as had his sister, in Westcliffe Heights.

He'd flown the nest. Moved out first.

Preston got out of the shower, dried his body, and wrapped a towel around his waist. As he was coming out of the bathroom and into his bedroom, he heard his cell phone ringing. Grabbing his phone, he saw his mother was calling.

He clicked the green button and proceeded to speaker so he didn't have to hold the thing as he dried and got dressed.

"Hey, Mom," he said.

"Hey, sweetheart."

"How are you doing, son?" this came from his dad, which made him smile.

"Hey, Dad, how are you?"

"I asked you first."

He chuckled. "I'm doing well. You know me. Constantly working."

"Yeah, I know, and that's what I don't like.

You've got to realize, young man, you're not going to be this age forever. There's nothing to life about working. Nothing at all. The world doesn't care if you do hundred-hour weeks with no life. They'll let you do it and not care about it."

"Greg, really, we both know he is not doing those hundred-hour weeks anymore. He's got himself a woman, and she is going to be taking care of him. There's no way she's going to want her man to spend all of his spare time at the office."

He couldn't help but smile, thinking of Eliza.

In the past few hours, he was pretty sure that was all she wanted to do. For him to spend every single waking minute in the office, far away from her.

"You're right. She is a peach. She doesn't want me working too hard."

"Where is she? Do I get to speak to her now?"

Shit. Fuck. Shit.

"Er, actually, Eliza is back at her own place."

Silence met his words.

"You're engaged, and you both still have your own place?" his mother asked.

Crap. This wasn't good. He'd been engaged to Eliza less than twenty-four hours and already he was fucking it up. His mother already sounded suspicious.

"Yes, we … we're both cautious. We do stay at each other's apartments. She's an independent woman. She likes to keep her own space."

He had no idea what he was talking about.

"Oh, well, I wanted you to know I got your old bedroom set up, and I've purchased fresh sheets. You and Eliza will be very cozy in that room."

"What about a spare room?" he asked. "Eliza doesn't want to embarrass you."

"Son, we've had five kids, and a whole fifty years

of loving one another. Believe me, we know what goes on between a man and a woman."

Of course, they did.

"I know, but this is … Eliza. She might prefer it, even if she doesn't use it."

"She is going to be family. Don't worry. I will talk to her and let her know that I know there is no better place than being with your man at night. Believe me, I wouldn't want to spend a moment away from mine." His parents chuckled.

"This is gross, guys. There has to be some law about parents making out at a time like this."

"Oh, stop your whining. When are you coming home?" his dad asked.

"I'll be with you Friday afternoon. There are a few things I've got to wrap up here, and then I'll be there. Back in my hometown, for a month." Back in his hometown for a month didn't bother him.

He did happen to love Westcliffe Heights. What he didn't like were his family's judgments.

His brothers, in particular, didn't understand his need to own his own company. To set out a life for himself in the city. They hadn't ventured far from home. Even when he gave them exclusive paid holidays abroad, they rarely cashed them in, preferring to stay local.

"I can't wait to meet Eliza," his mother said.

"She is looking forward to meeting you too." The lies fell off the tongue, and they were not fun, not in the slightest. He was going straight to hell for this.

"Tell me about her," his mother said.

"You want to know about Eliza? Like…"

"Everything about her. What she looks like. What she enjoys doing with her spare time. I don't know, tell me something that made my son sparkle."

He was screwed. "You know what, Mom, I will

tell you everything very soon, but I'm kind of, yeah, I need to, you know, get some sleep. I've got a busy day tomorrow, and I've got a whole lot of stuff to get organized."

"Right, of course. I'll say goodnight. Do you want me to sing you a bedtime story?"

"Nah, I'm good. Thanks, Mom." He wasn't a kid anymore.

She chuckled, as did his father. They were an act together, a complete riot.

He hung up the phone and realized without a shadow of a doubt, he needed to get Eliza and her little notebook together.

Chapter Four

Eliza didn't sleep.

Preston's assumption about her overthinking everything annoyed the hell out of her. She didn't overthink anything. Like an assignment back in college, there needed to be a good background. She was preparing for the worst.

"You look pissed," Juliet said.

She'd woken up an hour too early.

Glancing up at her friend, she noticed how perfect she looked. Not a single hair out of place. Her makeup wasn't too much, but enough to enhance the beauty of the woman beneath.

"Couldn't sleep."

"Do you want to talk about it?"

She slumped into her chair. "I think this ruse Preston wants me to partake on is headed for failure. You know how I feel about that."

"You are the anti-failure queen."

"I have never failed. I have always been ready and prepared. I don't think I can do this." She ran a hand down her face. She was so tired, and she'd gone without any kind of makeup. The chances of her smudging mascara onto her eyes were too damn high. She'd look like a clown.

Juliet placed a strong cup of coffee beneath her nose and the scent of the beans was already giving her a high.

"Have I told you how much I love you lately?"

"Nope, and certainly not enough."

They both chuckled, and she breathed in the scent of her coffee. "This is so good. I need this like an IV into my system right now." She took a sip, not caring that it burned as it went down. She needed all the help she could get.

"You shouldn't let this bother you. If your boss is ready and prepared, you've got this." She put a reassuring hand on her arm.

Smiling, she sighed. "You're right. I know I shouldn't care. It's not like I know his parents."

"You're going off a hunch?" Juliet asked.

"You two are losers first thing in the morning, you know that?" Mackenzie asked, coming out of her bedroom. She looked a mess. Her hair was a nest on top of her head. Her face had lines from a crumpled pillow, and she rubbed at her eyes as if she was still a child.

Eliza couldn't help but laugh at the pajamas she wore as she walked past them to get her own coffee, as one of the shorts had ridden up her ass.

"Your ass hungry today?" Eliza asked.

"Starved." Mackenzie pulled the shorts out and moved toward them. "What are we talking about at this time in the morning?"

It was like evolution had taken place in their kitchen. They were all different forms of the walking man from neanderthal. She wrapped her arms around Mackenzie. "I love you," she said.

"Love you too. You're still freaking out about your engagement to your boss?" she asked.

"Yep. Pretty much."

"If he's not worried and it's his family he's getting you to lie to, I'd just go with it, you know? You can't be held responsible if this goes pear-shaped."

"You're right, you're absolutely right, but once I set myself on a task, I have no choice but to complete it. You know how it is."

Mackenzie let her go, yawning with her mouth wide open, her eyes closed. "I don't believe it is even possible to think right now. I'm so tired. Today's the day."

"Possible takeover bid?" Eliza asked.

"Yep. It would seem Doug's Advertising will be no more in a few short weeks."

"Wait, hold up," Juliet said. "Since when did you go from having a suspected takeover bid to it being completely confirmed? What did I miss?"

"What did you miss? My boss's son finally got his father to agree that the best thing for the company is a buyout. The truth is he doesn't want to do any of the work. He's looking for a big payday, and the rest of us are just going to get passed over or fall with the ship. I'm already looking for a new job," Mackenzie said.

"You've been fired?" Eliza asked.

"No. I haven't been fired. You know I'm damn good at what I do, but I'm not going to sit on my ass and hope they don't fire me. You all know when a takeover bid like this happens that people are let go. I'm not going to be one of those women." She shrugged. "It's fine. I've got some money saved up for rent."

"Do not even go there, silly," Eliza said.

"Yeah, so not cool," Juliet said.

"We've got each other's backs. We have since we were kids. If you need time to get a job, then it's yours." Eliza wrapped her arms around her friend, and Juliet moved from behind the kitchen counter and hugged her best friend.

Mackenzie burst into tears. "I love you guys. I'm so sorry."

"Let it all out."

"I loved this job. You guys know I did. It was a lot of fun, and I was able to do my own thing, explore my creativity. A big company is going to try and squash me."

"They won't. Not if they know what is good for

them." Eliza kissed her friend's cheek.

Mackenzie pulled back and sniffled. "I'm good. I'm going to be good. It is all good."

They all started to laugh.

"I've got to head out," Juliet said. "You're going to be okay? We can do lunch?"

"Yes, lunch. No questions asked," Eliza said. "We are doing lunch."

They all agreed to meet at the Italian restaurant again. Mackenzie headed back to bed, and finishing her coffee, Eliza had no choice but to be the grownup and head out. She didn't take her car. Seeing as it was a lovely day, she started to walk toward her work.

It was only after the first hour passed and she realized she was going to be late that she signaled for a taxi.

With her cell phone in her hand, she quickly checked her work emails, surprised to find a massive email alert, as well as some sent to clients that were supposed to show up to meetings that day.

After paying the driver, she headed in, saying hello to the main receptionist as she ran toward the elevator.

She got to her desk just in time.

"Eliza," Preston said.

She let out a squeal, not expecting him near her desk. As she'd been about to sit down to find out who'd hacked into her emails, she missed the chair, throwing it back and landing on her butt.

"Ouch." She pursed her lips as pain ran up her spine.

"I'm so sorry. I didn't mean to startle you." He went to her side, offering her a hand.

"It's fine." She took his hand and he helped her to her feet. She rubbed at her ass, trying to soothe out the pain, and realized while she was holding the boss's hand and rubbing her ass at the same time.

To any onlooker, this would look way too strange.

She jumped back, colliding with her desk, nearly dropping the computer. She quickly grabbed it and sent whatever curse she could think of out to the klutz gods, to leave her the hell alone.

"Mr. Boone, I mean Preston, hi. Good morning, even. I just ... I think there is something wrong with the emails. There have been multiple sent that I've—"

He held his hand up, stopping her. "I sent them."

"You did?"

"Yes. I have access to every single account in this building."

"Right. Of course, you do. It's your company. It is only natural that you have full access to everything. It makes a lot of sense. Totally, a lot of sense." She was rambling now.

"Would you please step into my office?" he asked.

"Yes, of course. I still need to go and fetch your coffee and your breakfast."

"Already taken care of. I've been waiting for you to arrive."

"You got your own coffee and breakfast?" she asked.

"Of course."

She walked past him and pinched her arm. "Ouch!"

"Is your ... er ... bottom still hurting you?" he asked.

Eliza turned to see Preston with his hand poised close to her ass.

"What are you doing?" she asked.

"I … I thought you were in pain and I was going to rub it, and then I saw where it was and well …"

This was turning into a weird morning.

"Right, of course. I hurt my butt and you were going to rub it better." The words were coming out of her mouth, but they weren't helping this cause at all."

Preston stepped back. "You're not in pain."

"No, not in any kind of pain. I'm good. Fine. You know me, perfectly fine." Here she went rambling again.

She'd been working as Preston's PA for three years and not once did she have an incident like today. She was cursed. That was what this was. Purely cursed.

Pressing her lips together, she forced a smile. "So, what exactly did you want to talk to me about?" she asked.

Eliza turned back to the desk and saw the cups of coffees and two bagels.

"First things first. A coffee, no sugar, creamer."

"You know how I take my coffee?" she asked, amazed.

"It's a first. Also, I phoned the coffee shop and they told me what you liked."

"That makes more sense."

He placed the coffee in front of her. "The same with the bagel. Just a plain cream cheese."

"The way I like it." She forced a smile to her lips and watched him as he took a seat. This was strange. There was no other word to describe it.

"So, coffee and breakfast. What's the special occasion?" she asked.

He cleared his throat. "You are correct in your assumptions," Preston said.

"I'm correct in what assumptions?"

"To make this work, we're going to need to get to know one another. I need to know everything about you.

Your family. Your likes. Your dislikes. What makes you tick. Possibly even your menstrual cycle."

This made her cough. She quickly swallowed the piece of bagel in her mouth, nearly choking on it, then scolding her throat with the coffee as she forced it down.

"I'm sorry, menstrual cycle?" Her face was on fire.

"I know men are a little put off by it, but my mom raised her sons to be … well respectful of a woman's personal time, and that's what I'm doing. We're going to be away for an entire month, and during that time you will—"

"I know what will happen." This conversation couldn't get any weirder.

"I am sorry about all of this, and I do apologize. I hope you can forgo the sexual harassment complaint in the hope that you can see you'd be doing me a huge favor."

This was the closest thing she'd ever gotten to an apology from Preston Boone. She was going to take it.

"I know none of this is sexual harassment of any kind. We've got an arrangement, which includes talking very personal with each other. We can handle this. We're two grown adults, agreeing to a fake engagement for an easy and happier future."

She forced a smile to her lips. This was going to be easy.

Talking with her boss about her menstrual cycle, him knowing personal details about her. It was going to be a two-way street. There was nothing weird about this at all.

****

This was totally weird.

Preston couldn't even believe he'd put Eliza's cycle schedule in his calendar. When he was younger, and they were teaching sex ed at school, his mother had been strict with her boys to never make fun of a girl's time of the month. If she needed help or a young woman was showing signs of needing help, she expected her sons to be discreet and protective. In all his years, there was only one time, and that was with Annie Bilshaw, back in senior year. She'd … started her period, and rather than let the entire class make fun of her, he'd removed his sweater, wrapped it around her waist, and guided her out to her car.

He never got the sweater back, but what he did get was a giant thank you. She'd baked him a cake, and that was all he'd needed. No one needed to ever know that story, apart from his mom, who'd been so proud of him. Preston hadn't thought about that time in so long.

He rarely thought about Westcliffe as home, not anymore. The city was home, but at the same time, it wasn't exactly a comfort.

"I thought you told me not to overthink this," Eliza asked.

"You want to know these details now after you told me your menstrual cycle?"

She glared at him. "Personally, as a survival instinct, I think a boss should know every single woman's cycle. Then he gets to know when the best time to shut the hell up is."

He chuckled. "Right, is that PMS?"

"You're not funny, Preston."

"I'm hilarious." He smiled. "My mom called me last night. She wanted to know more about you, and then I realized other than being a damn good PA, the best I've ever had, I don't know anything about you."

She put her fingers behind her ear and smiled. "Come again. What did you say?"

"I don't know anything about you."

"You know that wasn't what I was getting at. I can take all compliments. Please do not skimp on any of them."

He smiled. "Fine. You're a damn good PA and you know it."

"I do."

"You know I was going to fire you, the next day," he said. "I realized how rash I'd reacted, and I didn't have the first clue about you. I thought it would be a bad fit."

"Then I should warn you that I'm allergic to failing. You gave me this job, and at first, I ran to the bathroom, had a panic attack, but then I got stuck in. I got to work, and I realized the order and I took over, making it even better," she said.

"You don't believe in failing?"

"No, sir. It's not in my blood to fail."

"I like that," he said.

"You should. It's what's going to help us." She brushed the crumbs off her fingers, folded up her napkin, and placed it in the trash.

Eliza reached for a spare notepad as well as a pen. "So we need to learn each other. You said you had three brothers. What are their names?" She had the pen poised over the notepad and then held her hand up. "Wait, we've got to be careful about this."

"Why?"

"If I know too much, then it will show I crammed for a test."

"We're engaged to be married. Doesn't that suggest we would've been going out long enough to know each other?"

"Long enough to know one another, but not long enough to have already met your mom, dad, and family. I met your sister just yesterday. Speaking of, where is she?"

"Headed back to Westcliffe Heights. She's done her deed for the day—ruin me."

"You're not ruined. We've got this. So I need to know enough that you'd tell your girlfriend that you were willing to marry, but not too much in the short time we'd been together. That seems fair, right?"

"It does seem fair."

"Great. Great. I like this," she said. "So three brothers. I'm thinking we stick to first names only. No one needs to know the middle name, and let's not go with age, but where they rank in terms of oldest to youngest."

"I'm the oldest, at forty."

"And I totally can know your age, because we're engaged." She started to write and stopped. "A ring. What are we going to do about a ring?"

"Already got it covered. After yesterday with my sister, I get to pick it up for lunch. I've already booked a table at the Italian place."

"Oh, I've arranged to meet my friends there," she said. "We are ... some of us ... we need to do lunch."

"Great. It will be a good opportunity for me to meet them, and learn more about them."

"You want to learn more about my friends?" she asked.

"Sure. Do they know this is an arrangement?" he asked.

"Actually, yes, they do. They also had your side and felt I was overthinking everything."

He smiled.

"That doesn't mean you were right."

"No, of course not," he said.

"We're sitting here now, cramming for a test on what we do and don't know about one another, Mr.

Boone, I mean Preston. Preston, it means that in this scenario, I was right."

"I'm not disputing that, Eliza. You were right and I wasn't. I am in total agreement."

She nodded. "Yes, you are. I will call and tell Mackenzie and Juliet that they'll be having lunch with my boss."

"Your fiancé," he said.

"Right, fiancé. That's totally normal. You would meet my friends before we got engaged. You're not just a boss."

He liked how nervous she was. She talked a hell of a lot more, which he did find cute. Very cute.

He sat back and watched as she called Juliet and then Mackenzie. After she hung up with the latter, she nibbled on her lip, a slight frown pulling between her brows.

"What is it?" he asked, concerned.

"Oh, it's nothing. You know. The same old. Same old."

"You're worried about them."

She put her cell phone away. "It is probably nothing to worry about at all. I know they can take care of themselves. They have been doing it for a long time, you know."

"It doesn't stop you from worrying any less."

"True. True. They're like the sisters I never had."

"An only child?"

"Yep."

He made a note. "So you're an only child and you went to college, I'm assuming with your three friends?"

"All correct. We've been living together ever since."

He made additional notes. "See. This isn't too hard."

"So for you, I've got your parents' names and your siblings. Is there any rivalry between them I need to know about? Any of them you don't get along with?" she asked.

"Nope. I'm good with all of them."

"Really?"

He lifted up from writing his notes. "Do you find it hard to believe I can be friends with my family?"

"Not that part, but I do find it hard you don't have any bets going or some competition with your brothers. That doesn't seem right."

He put his pen down. "We don't have any. I'm sure they have judgments of my lifestyle."

"Why would they have judgments?" she asked.

"Simple, I didn't want to stay in Westcliffe Heights, living off the Boone name. I felt compelled to make my own way in life," he said.

From a young age, he'd hated being told that the only reason he was successful was because of his family. He made it his mission to build this company from the ground up. No help from his father.

"You seem defensive," she said.

Without realizing it, he'd folded his arms. Quickly releasing them down to his sides, he forced a smile. "I'm fine."

"Okay, let's move on. You're all a happy family, got it." She kept her gaze on the notepad. "Anything else? Oh, I need those brothers' names," she said.

"Roger, Kian, and Andrew."

"Awesome. We're not going to go with middle names, just the first name. What about their spouses? Do you think we should talk about that?" she asked.

"All three are married, but would telling you their wives' names be something an engaged couple did?" He rubbed at his temple. Since when did organizing competent lies become so confusing?

She laughed. "How about we go with their first names, and we leave it at that? Kind of like a drop in the conversation."

He watched as she drew a line down all three names.

"Roger's wife is Lydia," he said.

She wrote it down.

"Kian is married to Grace."

"Pretty name."

"And Andrew is married to Scarlett," he said.

Eliza looked up.

"Is that going to be a problem for you to remember?" he asked.

"No, of course not." She made a note. "I think that's a good place to leave that. We don't want to delve in too deeply. It might look weird if I can write an essay on your family. What I need to know are all the intricacies that make you tick."

"You know I'm highly successful. I was the top of my class through college. I worked my ass on this place from the ground up. I'm extremely proud of what I've done. This is my home."

"You don't think of going back home to your folks?"

He opened his mouth to say he would never go home, but the words got stuck in his throat. He couldn't bring himself to say it.

Did he want to go back home?

Living in Westcliffe Heights wasn't a problem. It was home. It was where his family would be. The very thought of raising kids away from there seemed almost too ridiculous to comprehend.

"Can we move on?" he asked.

"You know we don't have to do this."

"I know, but the lies have already begun."

She shrugged. "You could tell your folks that you panicked and we could move it on from there. Tell them you wanted to impress them or something."

"Not happening." He leaned forward, glancing over his own list on Eliza. "You're an only child, and you don't see much of your parents right now. Why is that?"

"I'm working a lot," she said. "I talk to them as often as I can."

"Any bad blood between you guys?"

"None," she said. "They're good parents. They're nice and kind, and no way in hell do I want them to learn I'm fake engaged. We wouldn't be able to cancel. My mom would have us married off by the end of the month."

"She would?"

"My mom wants grandchildren."

"As does my mom. Do you not want kids?"

"Yes, of course, I do, but right now, I'm not ready to have them."

"How come?" he asked, intrigued.

She rolled her eyes. "Well, for one, I'm about to be fake engaged to my boss. I'm not seeing anyone, and if I was, I wouldn't agree to this. The list kind of goes on and on. Do you want me to continue?"

He held his hands up. "Nope. You're right. Kids are for stable relationships."

She chuckled. "I would say they're for people in love, or we can go with stable, but is anyone ever really stable?"

Preston looked at her, not sure if she was joking around or not.

"Kidding." She laughed. "Lighten up. At this rate, you're going to end up in an early grave and that wouldn't be good for anyone. Life is supposed to be fun, right? Living it up and all of that?" she asked.

"Yeah, you're right. Come on, let's get down to business."

He wanted all of these matters solved, and soon. When he finally visited his parents, he didn't want any slip-ups.

Chapter Five

Eliza was more than thankful for the break at lunchtime. Only, she was driving in Preston's car and they were heading back to the Italian restaurant, and her friends were going to be there.

She knew her besties would be on their best behavior, but she wasn't so sure about her boss.

This was ... surreal.

Learning about Preston was strange. First of all, he came from a large family, and even though she had some hint of this, she didn't exactly put two and two together and come back with this.

Not even close.

"Is there anything I need to know about your friends? Any ruse I need to keep up?" he asked.

"They know about what we're doing. I tell them everything. I don't keep secrets from them, ever."

"Ever?"

"Ever," she said. "They know we're doing this for your parents and also for Mr. Aguire. I'm so sorry about that. It just kind of slipped out."

"It's fine. I can imagine it was hard not to break the news to someone."

She glanced up and saw him smiling. It was rare for Preston Boone to smile. "Funny. You're a very funny guy."

They arrived at the restaurant, and Preston got out of the car. She opened her door, and he immediately moved the guy waiting to take the car out of the way, to hold her hand.

"I figured I may as well get used to this," he said.

She slid her hand into his, and she wanted to deny the electric current that went right up her arm, but it was impossible.

His touch felt … amazing.

Eliza pushed all those feelings to the back of her mind.

He was her boss. That was never going to happen. They had strict rules in place to guarantee it, and she wasn't going to be the one to break it.

The maître de took them to their seat where Mackenzie and Juliet already sat waiting.

"We only ordered drinks," Mackenzie said. "We didn't know how long you were going to be."

"That's totally fine. Everything is great. Er, guys, I'd like you to meet my boss and fiancé, Preston Boone. Preston, I'd like you to meet the charming Juliet and amazing Mackenzie."

He held out his hand, giving theirs a shake. "Charming to meet you."

Mackenzie and Juliet gave him the stink eye.

Taking her seat, she signaled the waiter. Instead of ordering tequila or something stronger, she opted for a water as a refreshment. Preston did the same.

"So, Preston, we hear you're engaged to our friend here," Mackenzie said.

He glanced at Eliza, looking a little unsure of himself.

"They know, okay? Don't let them fool you. They know that we're pretending." She rolled her eyes and turned toward them. "And they're just acting out their own little fantasy or whatever it is they're doing."

"We're taking care of our girl, and this is a good practice run," Julie said, looking at Mackenzie. "Don't you think?"

"I do think so. We need to make sure the guy who finally falls for our girl deserves her."

"I'm sure whoever falls for Eliza will be more than capable of taking you ladies on."

Juliet leaned on the table, leaning her chin on her open palms. "Is that right? And what kind of man does our girl need?"

"Someone who will love her no matter what. Someone who wants her to have everything her heart desires." He looked at her. "Someone who makes her happy."

"Damn, he's good," Mackenzie said. "Are you two sure this isn't the real deal?"

Eliza held up her finger. "No ring. This isn't the real deal. We're only pretending. All of this is fake."

"That's something you two are going to need to rectify, and you're also going to have to spend some time together," Juliet said.

This was news to Eliza. "Come again?"

"You've got 'til Friday to make this work. I get you guys pretending and doing your little assignments, but you should go and live with him for this next week."

Eliza laughed. Her stomach twisted. "That's crazy. We don't need to live together to pull this off."

"No? And what if you're observed? You don't know each other's bathroom schedule. What color her toothbrush is. This is stuff engaged couples know about each other. They've gotten past the nitty-gritty. They've seen each other at their worst and best. In fact, I suggest you guys go home and get wasted. Actually, you get wasted, and then you," Mackenzie said, pointing at each one in turn.

"You know, I thought you guys were crazy before and this just confirms it. We do not need to get wasted or live together to do this," Eliza said.

"Actually," Preston said. "It sounds like a good idea. It makes total sense."

"I like him," Juliet said.

"You like anyone who agrees with you," Eliza

said. "This isn't a good idea. We need our space. There's a chance we will kill each other."

"Precisely," Mackenzie said. "Which is why you need to do it. You're going to be with each other for an entire month. This isn't a weekend break, or being able to call in sick just to have time away from your boss. I'm not saying Eliza ever did that, but you guys get it. You know the drill. To make this work, you are both going to need to put in the effort. Eliza, my love, you hate failure. It would be an epic failure if his parents saw right through you. It would crush you."

She hated and loved her best friend with equal measure.

"She's right," Preston said. "To make this believable, even for Mr. Aguire, we're going to have to get the extra mile. After lunch, we'll stop by your apartment and you can gather your things."

"So, I've got to come and live with you. It can't be the other way around?"

"Nope. This is the only way."

She rolled her eyes. "I think it's time to eat. You two are banned from speaking. You've done enough damage."

Her friends smirked.

The waiter came and took their order. Eliza was starving, so she ordered a large plate of roasted tomato pasta. Anything to take the edge off. She also took a breadstick from the center of the table and started to eat it.

She needed carbs, and a brand-new common sense gene or whatever the hell common sense was supposed to be.

Living with her boss was just … wrong.

Their food arrived.

Preston had been merrily talking with her friends

about the world, some art piece, or whatnot. His cell phone rang, and he apologized, explaining he had to take it.

With him gone, she glared at her friends. "What the heck was that? You guys are supposed to have my back. Not be throwing me at him with lame excuses."

"Since when is failure a lame excuse?" Mackenzie asked.

"This is ... that's beside the point. You guys know how I feel about this." She growled. "It's not ... I cannot live with him."

"For the next week, you're going to have to. If this thing fails, which there is a big chance it will, we've got to live with you," Juliet said. "I hate living with you when you feel like a failure. All you talk about is being the biggest loser, and I love you way too much to let that happen. We've got your back. We're going to be a phone call away, and you never know, you might like being with him."

"He's my boss," she said.

"He's also hot," Mackenzie said. "There are worse people to spend your time with."

She didn't get a chance to make a comeback as Preston chose that moment to return. "Sorry about that." They ate their food, and Eliza let the conversation just drift from topic to topic.

Her friends were right.

She hated failure and would always spend way too much time analyzing her thoughts and her approaches. It was the one thing she hated more than anything in the world.

After their lunch, she hugged Juliet and Mackenzie tightly.

Following Preston out of the restaurant. They waited for the car, and once it arrived, he held the door open for her.

She thanked him, sliding inside. She'd put the seatbelt on as he got behind the wheel. Giving him her address, he pulled the car away from the curb.

"Your friends are nice."

"They're the best. No doubt." She loved them even as she hated them. They were both right though, and that was the pain in the ass she couldn't deal with.

Why did they have to be right?

They arrived at her apartment. Clearly, the fates had decided Preston was supposed to be with her today as there was a parking space outside. She lived in a nice neighborhood. With her, Juliet, and Mackenzie banding together, they were able to save up enough rent for a good place.

She climbed out of the car, totally aware of Preston joining her as they made their way into the apartment block. After traveling up the few flights of steps, she got to her door. The stairs seemed less intimate than the elevator. Her thoughts quickly drifted back to the strange moment at the elevator. How close he'd been, and she couldn't resist glancing at his lips, wondering how good they would feel brushing against her own.

She slid her key into the lock, flicked the door open, and stepped into her own world. The world she had away from the office. Her safe space. Her domain.

Invaded by her boss.

"Wow," he said, stepping inside.

"It's a nice apartment."

"You've got a lot of pictures," he said.

Over the years, Juliet, Mackenzie, and she had enjoyed a lot of time together. Making so many memories. They had pictures of reminders of the adventures they shared. On the far wall was a picture of the three of them together, arms across each other's shoulders, smiling at the camera. It was taken during a camping trip. Mackenzie's dad had donated the tent for them to take out into the woods.

They hadn't lasted the whole night as they thought they heard wolves and bears. They ended up using their sleeping bags and flashlights in her own folks' living room. After that night, they agreed to never go on a camping trip.

"We wanted to document everything. It seemed important to us."

He lifted a picture. "And this?"

She moved toward him. "That was the day we moved into this apartment. We'd all gotten jobs, and we felt like was going to be a huge success."

"You don't think it is?"

"I'm fake engaged to my boss," she said. "I think I'm doing well. I'm going to pack a few things. Make yourself at home."

She rushed into her bedroom, not wanting Preston to get too comfortable with everything. Grabbing two bags, she went to her closet and looked at the ready-made clothes she'd purchased on the high street, and the few garments she made.

Her mother's hobby was that of a dressmaker. She loved to sew and craft, and Eliza had picked it up, but she never talked about it. Her best friends encouraged her to make more, but between work and everything else, she didn't have the time. Her sewing machine was wrapped up in the corner of her room.

Ignoring it, she packed her clothes, some lingerie, and some shoes. She didn't bother to pack any books or to do anything else.

With her bags packed, she entered the main sitting room. Preston sat there, looking around the room. "Your place is ... homely," he said.

"I guess you can never take the town out of the girl," she said. "I like to feel at home wherever I go. I'm ready."

"You packed light?"

"Nope, I packed prepared."

****

Entering his apartment, Preston became aware of how sterile his space looked in comparison to Eliza's.

Her small apartment was lived in. It was alive with memories, of a family. They were three best friends, but he knew without a shadow of a doubt they were also a family. Just looking at the pictures alone, he knew they were a unit.

He'd witnessed it at lunch, but her apartment confirmed that.

His place had no real personal touch. This was just somewhere he used to crash away from work. No special pictures. No sign of a real person living here.

He held Eliza's bags as he insisted on carrying them for her. "So, this is my place."

"I've been here before," she said.

"Yeah, I know. Of course, I know. I'll show you to your room." He had a spare room always made up. Trudy, his sister, usually stayed, but she hadn't stuck around this time. Nope, she'd thrown him to the wolves and allowed them to feed on his corpse. So much for a nice sister.

It kind of pissed him off.

No, it didn't kind of do it. It did.

He knew Trudy had a plan, and he was going to have to figure it out, but until then, he was on his own.

The bedroom was large with a king-sized bed in the center. "The en-suite is through there. Let me know if you need anything. Towels or a toothbrush. Stuff like that."

"Yeah, okay. Sure. Fine. Cool. This is totally fine. We can do this, Preston."

"You're nervous," he said.

"A little bit. It's not every day you live with your boss. This will be fine because we know what we're doing, right? Totally right. This is going to be a breeze."

"We're screwed if you're nervous right now." He didn't have the heart to tell her they'd be sharing a room.

That revelation could come on the day.

"So, I'll be waiting for you in the sitting room," he said.

"Yeah, sure," she said. "I'll be out in a second."

He left her to put her stuff away, going back to his main sitting room with his blank walls and black furniture. The eligible bachelor pad.

When he first moved in, he'd been proud, almost impressed with what he accomplished. Now, after seeing Eliza's place, he saw an empty carcass.

After going to his liquor, he poured himself a shot of whiskey.

"You're doing the drunken thing today?" she asked. "That makes sense. This is your apartment." She'd joined him, and he saw she still wore her office uniform.

"I'm just enjoying a drink. Want to join me?" he asked. "I don't think we need to get wasted."

"No, I don't think getting wasted would be a good idea."

He poured her out a glass of his finest whiskey.

She took a sip and her nose wrinkled, but she swallowed. "Oh, my, what is that?"

"Expensive," he said.

"You need to contact your supplier. It tastes like mold. That is so gross." She didn't hand him back the glass.

"Do you want to sit?" he asked.

She perched on the edge of the sofa, and he sighed, sinking back.

His furniture was so fucking stiff!

He'd sunk into Eliza's sofa. It had been so soft and welcoming.

"Maybe you can tell your parents that I died? Or that I had a twin and she'd been bamboozling you since I left town. I vanished?" Eliza asked.

"I could do all of those things, or you could attempt to relax, and we just talk, like normal people. No notes. No planning. Just talk," he said.

He'd already begun to get a headache at the back of his mind.

"Yeah, you're right." She took a sip of her whiskey. "We can do this, even with your bad taste in alcohol."

"So, what is your poison of choice?"

"When the time calls for it, tequila."

"A guaranteed hangover."

"Yep, and I've sworn off it for life. Last time I drank it, I ended up engaged to my boss."

He couldn't help but burst out laughing. "So that was why you were late."

"Yep. My alarm decided not to go off, and Juliet didn't know, so no wake-up call from her. You get the drill," she said. "It was a morning of disasters. No coffee place. No breakfast. The world was against me, and then I'm suddenly engaged. I snagged a rich man all by being a screwup." She smiled at him. "That's the way it looks."

"Very true. You're not a screwup, though. You've been the most competent assistant I've ever had," he said.

"Wow, that stuff is strong if you're already paying compliments."

"I know when I've got a good employee, and you,

Eliza, are damn good." He lifted his glass toward her in salute.

"If we're being all honest and stuff, then you should know you're not a bad boss, at all. You're pretty great, actually."

"I am?"

She chuckled. "Don't let it get to your head, but I do know you take care of your employees. Your company means everything to you, and I can see that."

"I'm a workaholic."

"Yes, you are. You got to learn to live a little. None of us want anything bad to happen to you, you know. When you gave me this job, I was so freaking scared. I was excited as well. Obviously. My very angry boss had just come and pointed a finger at me and said you're my new PA. It was an opportunity of a lifetime. I took it. Most of the time, I like this job."

"When don't you like this job?" he asked.

She shook her head. "I'm not going to tell my boss when I don't like my job."

"We've got to be real with each other, and your job is guaranteed," he said.

"Yeah, but only if I stick with being your fiancée. Not that there's any kind of pressure."

He sighed. "There's no pressure. My folks, if not my brothers or my sister, are going to ask these kinds of questions. It would be nice to know what you'd say."

She turned a little toward him.

He had never noticed the sharp blueness of her eyes before. They were so clear, such a pretty color. They were not like the ocean at all. They were far more mesmerizing than the waves.

"When we don't land a client," she said. "When a deal goes bad, you're ... moody. Not like a petulant child or anything like that, but you're not happy, and I know you're not happy, you know." She sighed. "I think that is the hardest part. I want to help you. It kind of drives the whole feeling of failure up a notch."

"You can't control every single part of your life."

"Exactly, but that doesn't mean I don't want to. Believe me, I do want to, like all the time." She sighed. "There's always so much going on. I love that."

"You love being busy."

"Don't you? Back home, I used to work as a waitress in this dying diner. They hadn't changed their menu in like fifty years. A brand-new diner, one that was willing to experiment, opened up, and there was no one coming to this old diner for days. I think old man Hubert liked that. He wanted to see his diner die. Eventually, he closed up, but I was so bored."

"You get a job at the new diner?"

"No, I went away to college after that," she said with a smile. "I'm a loyal person. I wouldn't work for a rival diner. I wouldn't work for a rival firm either, Preston. In case you were ever worried about that."

He put his hand on top of hers. "I don't think I've earned such loyalty."

"It doesn't matter if you earned it or not. I'm giving it. You do good work."

"You think buying companies, breaking them down, building them up, or completely removing them is good work?" he asked.

"Okay, fine. Not everything you do is good work. I imagine you have a reason for it. You do keep good companies though. You can't deny that."

He sighed. "Can I be honest with you?"

"I'm your fake fiancée. If you can't be honest with me, who can you be honest with?"

"There are times I hate my job," he said.

She frowned. "Preston, you created this company.

How can you hate it?"

"Back home, I watched my dad sink good money into bad businesses all because he didn't want to see them go under. Rather than tell the people who owned them that they needed to adapt their business model, or just close the shit down. I would get angry because he didn't give them the truth. He allowed them to believe they had a great company. I decided that when I was old enough, I was going to make the right decisions for each company. I'd assess whether it was viable to keep it or to throw it away. Sometimes, the best thing about a company is the people within it. Their ideas need to be protected."

"You saying that makes me think of Mackenzie. Doug's Advertising has been taken over. In the next few weeks, she will get to find out if she's being replaced."

"There's always a job for her at our place," he said.

She laughed. "Mackenzie would hate it. Deep in her core, she's an artist. Working in corporate would kill her."

"I'll find a place for her to thrive."

"Thank you." Eliza put her other hand on top of his. "You know, your dad isn't wrong to keep on investing in places. You probably don't want to hear it, but there was a time when each company was doing well. It's why they become lifelong names, especially in small towns. Big business infects small towns, drives the small shop away, and in doing so, you lose something."

"Is this how you tell me you hate my company?" he asked.

"I don't hate it because in the companies you save, you don't make the changes on the inside. You spruce it up a little, provide the necessary training and services to the staff, and you help to build it up. You're more like your father than you probably realize."

He couldn't deny that his father was a good man.

They sat in silence.

Preston reflected on the arguments he had with his father growing up. The old DIY place, he'd been so angry when his father had invested yet thousands of more dollars into nothing.

"And what, you think our town isn't worth it? You think the people who call themselves Westcliffe Heights isn't worth it?"

"Dad, you are wasting good money after bad. If he can't stay afloat, then tell him to sell his business. There is plenty of investment—"

"Opportunities. I'm very much aware of what kind of investment opportunities are in my own town, Preston Boone. It would be easier, wouldn't it? Turn everyone away. Tell them all no, they are on their own. They can't stay afloat and money doesn't grow on trees. So they sell up their land to a let's say a property investor. One by one, they all fall, and it won't be long until Westcliffe Heights is nothing more than a stomping ground to mall activity. I've seen what happens, and that kind of life isn't welcome in this town. We're a community that takes care of each other. Not some statistic men look over to see how much additional money they would make."

Their arguments had continued for years.

They never talked about his company or what he did.

Preston couldn't help but wonder if his father would be happy with him or ashamed. The city life was great for so many reasons, but it wasn't home.

Why was he starting to realize that?

Chapter Six

"You eat chocolate chips in your pancakes?" Preston asked.

"You have yours with a banana mashed into it. Believe me, yours is gross, mine is delicious." She lifted her forkful of fluffy chocolate chip pancakes and took a bite. She closed her eyes. "So good."

They were eating breakfast. Preston was dressed in a suit, while she'd entered his kitchen in pajamas. Her hair wasn't done. She'd washed her face and brushed her teeth, but hunger had struck.

She'd been mixing up the batter for her pancakes when Preston joined, requesting a mashed-up banana.

Now they had their coffees and were enjoying breakfast at his long dining table. She sat next to him while he was at the head of the table. She didn't know when he'd gotten his newspaper.

It was a Sunday morning.

No work, but he was dressed for work.

"Are you heading into the office today?" she asked.

"No, I'm not."

"So why are you dressed so ... worky?"

"Worky? That's not a word."

"It is now, and I said it." She put another piece of pancake into her mouth.

"This is how I dress."

"You never just hang out, and I don't know, enjoy yourself?" she asked.

"I do."

"What do you normally do on a Sunday?"

His eye twitched.

"You do, don't you?" she asked. "You work on a Sunday."

"I catch up on some emails and do some research."

"Do you not know how to have fun at all?"

"I'm eating pancakes with you."

She rolled her eyes.

"What do you usually do?" he asked.

"Hang out with my friends. We sometimes watch movies. Cook. Mackenzie isn't allowed to cook though. She cannot cook if her life depended on it. If it's nice out, we take a picnic out to the local park. It's always busy, but it's fun." She shrugged. "We do whatever we fancy, unless my demanding boss requires me to send him files. Sunday is a slob day." She pointed at her pajamas.

When she saw him enter the kitchen, her first instinct was to run and change into her suit, but she'd squashed it. Preston needed to get used to her in pajamas.

"The pancakes are good."

"Come on, go get changed out of your suit," she said. "You've got to be uncomfortable being in that thing. It's so hot outside."

The sun was already up. She'd found his AC unit and turned it on.

He glanced down at himself. "There's nothing wrong with the way I'm dressed."

"I didn't say there was anything wrong, and there isn't, but come on. You are not working today."

"I'm about to be away from my company for the next month."

"Mr. Boone, I already have everything in place and ready. We are on constant call, and I'll have the necessary means of hooking you up in case of an emergency meeting. I will not fail you. I have never failed you, but you need to go get changed into something. I'm going to take you out, and you're going to learn to live a little."

She pulled him to his feet and moved him toward his bedroom. Her hands were on his back, and she was not staring at his tight ass. Nope. Nor was she paying attention to how firm he felt beneath her hands.

Touching Preston was a strange experience. She'd been working with him for three years, and in all that time, she had failed to ever touch him.

How was that possible? To never touch someone you worked closely with?

"Get dressed. I will meet you out here in five minutes," she said.

"You're telling me it is only going to take you five minutes to get dressed?" he asked.

"Yep."

"I doubt that."

"Are you making a bet?" she asked, hands on hips.

He folded his arms. "I am."

"Okay, fine. If I'm ready in five minutes, you hang out with me the whole day as Preston, not my boss. If you win, and I take longer, then we can do work 'til your heart's content."

"I will take that bet." He held out his hand, she shook it, and he took off his watch. "The time is set. Go."

She ran to her bedroom.

What Preston didn't know was prior to leaving her bedroom, she had already pulled out the clothes she intended to wear for her slob Sunday. A pair of loose-fitting shorts, a long shirt, and a pair of open-top sandals.

She moved quickly, changing into panties and a bra, sliding on her shorts, and pulling her shirt over her head.

Next, she ran a brush through her hair, wincing at the knots, but pushing on through. After tying her hair on top of her head, there was no time for makeup, and she was being real. A Sunday never required makeup.

Feet in her sandals, she was out at the spot where Preston was waiting. His mouth hung open.

"I guess I'm the one in charge for today," she said.

"You cheated."

"No. I even have underwear on." She winked at him. "Go get dressed for a walk in the park, my friend."

He was dumbfounded.

"Oh, I think it might help you to know that for fun, Mackenzie, Juliet, and I would time ourselves getting changed. It would pass the time, and guess who was always the winner."

"You ... you knew you'd win."

"I don't believe in failure, boss, or should I say, Preston."

He disappeared, and she laughed.

Pulling out her cell phone, she saw her besties had texted her goodnight and good morning.

Dialing their apartment, she waited for them to answer.

"Hello," Juliet said.

"Hey, it's me. Just wanted to see how you both were doing on this fine Sunday. You know, you could see me if it hadn't been for you guys giving this insane idea to my boss about me and him pretending to fake live together to be fake engaged."

Juliet snorted. "There's nothing fake about you living together. For the next month, you guys will be living together, in close proximity with his parents. You know this is a good plan."

She sighed. "You're right, and I hate it. Where's Mackenzie?"

"Still sleeping."

"Really?" She checked the time. "It's nine-thirty."

"And she pretty much passed out last night. I think this takeover-job thing is bugging her more than we realize."

"Do you need me to come over?" she asked.

"Nope. I've got Mackenzie covered. I've already baked her banana bread. Her favorite."

Eliza wrinkled her nose. "I do not know what is with you guys and your obsessions with bananas. They're disgusting."

"They're tasty, and you know it."

She liked a banana, but in baked food, that was taking it too far.

"What are you doing today?" Eliza asked. They would always agree to disagree when it came to the use of bananas.

"We're going to pig out, watch a few movies. Talk about you."

"Oh, yay, I better be awesome in your gossip. How I make the most difficult sacrifices."

"Actually, I think we're going to talk about what a giant pain in the ass you are. How you never make any sacrifices." Juliet burst out laughing. "Sorry, I couldn't even finish that sentence. Okay, all joking aside. How are you holding up?"

"Let's see, I'm in a blank canvas of an apartment. I think they used this place to film horror movies. My boss does nothing but work, but that's a given. He loves mashed-up banana in his pancakes. How do you think it is going?"

"Ouch, that bad?"

"It's not bad, per se. It's just, I don't know, it's weird, you know."

"This is what you get for screwing your boss."

"I'm not screwing him. Believe me, that's not happening."

"But you've got to pretend to be doing him," Juliet said. "Engaged couples are supposed to be close. Having-sex-on-every-single-surface-of-their-apartment kind of close."

She snorted. "Not all engaged couples are horny for one another. Some have a mutual respect for one another's mind."

"Oh, please. You don't fool me, Eliza Drake. You and I both know that when you find a guy to be engaged to, he has to be passionate. They were the rules of you getting married, remember?"

"You promised never to bring that up," Eliza said. "We all promised."

"Actually, we didn't. What we did as kids was promise we wouldn't tell any potential boyfriend who didn't meet all of the desired requirements. I never told your ex that he was a loser in bed. Nor did I tell him he had weird pancake things." Juliet gasped. "Preston has one of your points."

"Do not go there."

"Come on, Eliza, work with me right now. Preston loves weird pancakes. As a kid, that's what you said. Do you remember what you said?"

"I'm going to hang up now. What you're saying makes no sense." She hung up her cell phone and shoved it in her pocket.

"My man is going to have weird taste in pancakes. Maybe even have crushed-up banana or tea pancakes."

"Why does he have to have weird pancake taste?" Juliet asked.

"So we have parts of ourselves that are different. Two souls need to have differences to match on other levels."

Eliza remembered many on her list of a suitable partner, and she wasn't going to think of any of them right now.

This thing with Preston wasn't a real engagement. It didn't matter that he liked strange pancakes. That was just one thing on her list.

"How does this work?" Preston asked.

Eliza smiled. He'd dressed in a pair of shorts and a pale-blue button-up shirt. He looked ... like an old frat boy.

"I ... like the look."

"Really?"

"Why not? Come on, let's go." She grabbed his arm, marching him out the apartment building. They went to the elevator, but she didn't go to the underground parking garage, instead, straight to the main floor.

"I don't like this. You don't want me to drive you anywhere?" he asked.

"We can drive later. For now, we just need to walk. You've got to learn to take in the sights of everything that surrounds you."

They left his apartment building, but they weren't breathing in clean, crisp air.

Sounds of cars honking, and the chaos of the roads was very clear to see. The streets were already busy.

Fortunately, with her arm through his, she walked him down the streets. Preston had such a commanding presence, and no one walked in front of him.

Eliza didn't like how long it took her to get to the park, but the moment they arrived, she saw she wasn't the only one to enjoy a morning walk early in the morning.

After she grabbed Preston's hand, they entered the gate and immediately had to move as a biker dinged his bell to alert them to his presence.

"Just when you think you love the city, it has a nasty habit of reminding you exactly why you hate it," Eliza said.

"Coffee?" he asked.

"Yes, let's go for coffee."

They left the park and found a small little café. Eliza got a small table for them outside, and as she looked at the city now, she couldn't help but be critical. Her mother had once told her that life had a nasty way of running away from you. If you were too busy chasing a future rather than living in the present, you'd find yourself in places you didn't want to be in.

She rubbed at her arms. For the first time since moving to the city, she felt homesick.

"You okay?" Preston asked.

"Yeah, I'm fine. Do you ever find that you hear your mother's voice at the most inopportune moments?" she asked.

"That I do."

****

Their Sunday wasn't a total disaster. They never made it to the park, and after sitting at the café, Preston was aware of Eliza's sadness. He didn't know what caused it, but the truth was, after being out in the city on a Sunday, he was feeling it too.

Growing up in a small town, he knew Sunday was a day to be with family. To have large dinners, to laugh, to dance, to have fun.

With his years in the city, he hadn't thought about the times he shared back home. He didn't know what Eliza was doing to him, but whatever it was, it wasn't good. She reminded him of home, of his family. Her apartment had set it off.

His parents were going to love her.

She was all about friends and family, he saw that.

She was also hardworking and loyal. All good traits, which was why on Monday, they were back in the office, working hard, and he was distracted. They had canceled all his meetings, and he was working his ass off to be ready for the next month, but he kept glancing at Eliza.

His thoughts should be focused on the work at hand, not his beautiful PA.

Glancing up, he saw her as she leaned over her desk, grabbing a pen while she was on the phone. In between talking, she wrote down a note, and then typed on her computer.

She wore a pastel-blue suit that seemed to enhance the golden hue of her hair.

He'd seen her during her downtime, in her pajamas, eating pancakes. Running fingers through his hair, he tried to focus on the work at hand. Looking at Eliza was not getting work done.

Preston stared down at the contract in his hand.

You're going to focus on work.

Eliza is fake.

You're not in a relationship with her.

She knocked on his office door, and he looked up.

"So, a Melissa called. She asked if you were still on for dinner tonight as you hadn't called her?"

He frowned.

Eliza came and put the note down on the desk, in front of him.

"Crap, I forgot to cancel her."

"Yeah, er, just to be clear, I may be playing the part of fake fiancée, and I have no problem with you ... doing your thing, but while we're playing our parts, please, don't make me look like a fool."

"No ... girlfriends," he said.

"If you don't mind." She pointed her pen at him. "Why don't you call that Melissa and ask her to play that fiancée role instead?"

"Hell, no. Melissa was a mistake. I had every intention of canceling on her." He had no interest in Melissa. She was a journalist, intent on making her way up in the world. She had tried to get him into bed, but he'd taken her out to dinner, arranged another date, and took her straight home.

No sex.

No kisses.

He hadn't been interested and he'd forgotten about the rearranged dates.

"Well, if it makes you feel any better, do you want me to give her the fiancée treatment?" Eliza asked.

"What kind of treatment?" he asked, sitting back.

"I can tell her that it would be in her best interest to not talk to you or contact you as you are presently engaged."

"Melissa is a journalist. I tell her that, she's going to want to know who I'm engaged to. This would take our ruse to a whole new level."

Eliza opened her mouth. "Ah. You see, this is why you're the boss and I work underneath you."

He had a very different image of how she would look underneath him.

"I mean besides you. You know what I mean."

He chuckled. "I do. You can still cancel this appointment for me, and after you've done that, do you want to go to lunch?"

"You want to leave the office again for lunch?"

"I think while our fake engagement is in play, the less time we spend in the office, the better." He glanced past her shoulder.

"Crap," she said. "We haven't talked about how

we're going to be in the office." She quickly rushed toward the door, closing it. "Do you think anyone knows?"

"You're the one who would get all the office gossip," he said.

"I haven't heard a thing." She wrinkled her nose. "So, we can totally do this. We can pretend to be nothing to each other, while also being engaged, and crap, this is so not going to work. I'm exhausted just thinking about it." She collapsed into the chair. "What are we going to do?"

"Simple, while at work, we deny everything. We're going to be engaged at Westcliffe Heights. Mr. Aguire will see us there. There will be no reason for it to extend into the office."

"Apart from where we're seen arriving together?" she asked, brows raised.

"Good point. So how about I drop you off a few blocks from work?" he asked.

"We can do that. See, we can problem-solve. We got this."

Eliza got to her feet and left his office.

He wasn't checking her ass out as she left.

They got through the rest of their morning, went to lunch, and Eliza took him to a hot dog stand. He hadn't eaten a hot dog since he was a kid back at home. It tasted good, but he knew his mother would do them better.

Why was he missing home so much now?

He'd loved how different the city life was to home life. This was a different kind of chaos to back home.

They finished their lunch, and he didn't know how Eliza did it, but she managed to keep the conversation based on work.

Once in the office, he kept an eye on people, wondering if they were gossiping about his private life. Eliza went about her work, and he found himself attuned to her whereabouts. He noticed whenever she left her desk or was just sitting there working.

He relished the moments she walked into his office, with notes or documents for him to sign.

The day went by so slowly, and he was bored with work. Thinking about home.

Eliza came to his office at five. "I'm going to head out for the night. I figured I'd walk a few blocks, and you could pick me up."

She mentioned a Chinese takeout place, and he promised to pick her up in fifteen minutes.

He finished off some more work, got all the necessary details he'd need, and then closed down for the evening.

There was no one around to stop him as he made his way to the parking garage. After climbing behind his wheel, he pulled out and found Eliza waiting, carrying a small box of food. The moment she climbed into the car, he felt his stomach growl.

"You're hungry?" she asked.

"Starving."

"Take us back to your place."

He pressed his foot to the gas, but he didn't break any speed limits.

Preston pulled out his keycard that would allow him access to the underground parking lot. Finding his spot, he pulled up, and then Eliza was already climbing out of the car. They walked to the elevator.

He stepped inside with her. The doors closed, and he couldn't help but watch her.

She stood, holding the box.

"Here, let me take that," he said.

"It's fine. It's not too heavy."

"My mom always taught me to be the perfect gentleman. I'm not going to stop now." He took the box from her as the elevator doors opened. "My key is in my pocket."

She slid her hand within his pocket, and it was so close to his dick that he tensed up. Eliza didn't seem to notice as she opened the apartment door.

"I'm sorry. My feet are killing me." She kicked off her shoes, losing a couple of inches in height as she flexed her feet.

He kicked his door closed, and Eliza was behind him, locking the door.

Another difference between his hometown and city. Locking doors.

Get a grip.

He couldn't keep making comparisons. He loved the city life.

"Do you want to take that to the table?" she asked. "I'll grab some forks."

"What about plates?"

"You eat takeout food on plates? The whole point is not to do dishes?"

"Then no plates."

He carried the food to the table, and Eliza joined him with a couple of bottles of beer and two forks. They were just starting to eat when his cell phone rang.

Pulling it out of his pocket, he groaned. "It's a video chat with my parents."

"Okay. Do you want me to leave?" she asked, already getting to her feet.

He grabbed her arm. "No. No. You stay. They can meet you tonight," he said.

"That sounds fair." She nibbled on her lip.

"It will be fine. They're my parents," he said as a

way of explanation.

"Of course, they're your parents. It will all be fine. Totally fine." She ran her fingers through her hair.

"You look great," he said.

"Yes, thank you. You look great as well."

He accepted the call. "Mom. Dad, hey," he said.

"What's wrong, Preston?" his mother, Marsha said.

"Nothing. Nothing at all. I'm just surprised by your call."

"He's surprised. Hey, big bro," Andrew said, coming into view.

"When are you going to get your ugly butt down here?" Trudy said.

"The whole gang is there," he said.

"No, the whole gang is not here because you're not here," Kian said.

"They're all excited to meet your fiancée, sweetie. We all are. It's not every day that your eldest son brings a girl home."

"Mom, you have three sons, married. They did one better than Preston," Trudy said.

"I know. I know. They are all married and have given me grandchildren, but you all know how I worry about Preston."

If he wasn't careful, she was going to start crying, saying how he was always fighting settling down. He grabbed Eliza's hand, giving her no choice but to lurch toward him, where he moved so that she sat on his knee.

As an employer and employee, this was deeply inappropriate. As an engaged couple, this was normal.

Silence rang out on the line, and Eliza sucked up the noodles she'd been starting to slurp up.

"Everyone, I want you to meet Eliza Drake. My fiancée. Eliza, this is all of my crazy family I've been telling you about."

He heard her swallow. She held up her hand. "Hi, everyone."

Silence.

He'd never known his family to be so silent before. Maybe he should spring fiancées on them more often. He rested his hand on Eliza's hip, becoming increasingly aware of how full it was.

"Eliza, honey, we had no idea that Preston was so serious," Martha said. "Oh, Greg, look, she's so beautiful."

Eliza cleared her throat, putting the carton of noodles onto the table. He watched her grab a napkin and discreetly wipe at her mouth.

"Preston has told me so much about you. I can't wait to meet you all."

"Yeah, we can't wait to meet you. You'll be a new little sister in the house. What are you, twelve?" Kian asked.

He growled at his brothers.

"I will take that as a joke and not an insult," Eliza said. "I'm twenty-nine. Not that big of an age gap."

"Boys, enough, enough. I want to talk more with my new daughter-in-law," Marsha said.

"Mom, we're not married yet. You're going to scare her off."

"No, I'm not. She looks like a woman who doesn't scare off easily. Am I right, Eliza?"

"You'll be the first mother I've met."

Preston turned to look at her.

"Now that surprises him. See, Preston is surprised," Trudy said. "Trouble in paradise already?"

"No trouble at all," Preston said. "At this rate, you're all going to be lucky to even get the chance to meet her if you scare her off."

There was some more commotion and before too long, his brothers and sister were out of the line of the camera. His parents sat, similar to how he was with Eliza. His mother in his father's lap.

"You are coming? There isn't going to be some last-minute cancelation or you finding another reason to cancel on us?" she asked.

"Mom, I told you, I didn't mean to cancel all of those times. I was busy. Work got in the way."

"It is always work, work, work with you. Son, we miss you," Greg said.

"I'm coming home, and you're going to get to meet Eliza." The conversation was becoming more stilted with each word spoken. "I've got to go. I'll talk to you soon." He ended the call. "Sorry about that."

"You don't have to apologize. You might want to let me go so I can get off your lap. You probably have a dead leg."

He didn't want to let her go but chose not to make a scene, removing his hand from her thigh.

"Do you want to talk about it?" she asked.

"No, I really don't."

"Then we won't talk about it." She picked up her noodles. "Let's eat."

Chapter Seven

Friday morning

"So, what's the plan?" Juliet asked.

Eliza finished her piece of bacon and looked between Juliet and Mackenzie. This was the first meal they had shared with each other all week since they became the enemy and sent her off to live with Preston.

"He's coming to pick me up from here. I wanted to say goodbye to you guys. Make sure we're still friends before you attempt to get rid of me." She pouted.

"Come on, how was living with your boss?" Juliet asked.

"It was ... fine."

"She's gritting her teeth."

She sent another glare toward Mackenzie. "I didn't want to live with him. I've never lived with a man ever."

"But you also never pretended to be engaged to one either," Juliet said. "Don't you feel more prepared to meet his parents now than before?"

She thought about the video call with his family and the truth was, no, she didn't feel more prepared. "No, I don't. I feel so far out of my depth. His family is close to him. You can see that, but I don't know, I think there are a few problems at home."

"They're abusive?" Mackenzie asked.

"No, no. Nothing like that. It's hard to explain. It's like..." She paused and frowned, glancing around the café they'd picked. It was a nice, down-to-earth place, with white walls and a brown border. Tartan cloth covered each table and the waitresses each wore an oval half-apron. She liked the family feel of the café. It reminded her a little of being back home.

All this talk of families and going back home had

started to make her realize how much she missed her own home. "It's like his family isn't happy with him going out on his own. I could be wrong. From what I know, the Boone name is a big deal back in Westcliffe."

"He's going to be a celebrity?" Juliet asked.

"Probably. I can't help but wonder if there is going to be a spiteful ex in the woodwork, you know?"

"Maybe she will try to murder you and Preston will save you. You'll get married for real and have little genius babies," Mackenzie said.

"Where did that come from?" Eliza asked, laughing.

"I don't know. I've got a hundred bucks that you fall in love with Preston."

She looked toward Juliet, who held her hands up as if she was innocent.

"I've got a hundred bucks that Preston falls in love with you, but he does something stupid and he has to come and grovel."

Eliza rolled her eyes. "Guys, you are putting way too much stock into this. We all know this is going to end badly. Preston is going to look like the lying bad guy. I'm probably going to look like a gold-digging whore. I'll lose my job. His business will get sold or torn apart, and we'll ruin everyone's lives. I'll turn to drink, and you'll bury me before I'm forty."

Juliet gasped. "Or, you both fall madly in love but he has to go away to war, and you are pregnant with his baby, and he comes home to discover the love of his life has moved on."

"I have no idea what movie that's from," Eliza said.

Mackenzie laughed. "I'm not thinking of movies. I'm overdramatizing what is going to happen."

"I hate you both," Eliza said. "I'm going to miss

you guys. You'll call me every night?"

"Nope, we're not stalkers," Juliet said. "We'll call you twice a day. Once in the morning, once in the evening. I vote on Code Crap. You say that, we give you a reason to get the hell out of dodge, or we come down there."

Eliza got up and went to her friends, hugging them tightly. "This is crazy what I'm doing. You know that, right?"

"Totally crazy, but you've got to admit, it's kind of fun," Mackenzie said. "I hope you guys do fall in love. You and Preston look great together."

She hadn't told them about how he'd pulled her onto his lap so they could talk to his parents. How it was a struggle for her to follow the conversation because she was sure he stroked her hip.

It was always the little touches that did it for her. The light stroke or gentle caress.

She hugged Juliet, then Mackenzie, then both at the same time. This was the longest they had ever been apart.

Out the window of the café, she saw Preston park his car. Her bags were already packed and ready. He said if she needed anything else, he'd take her shopping.

All she wanted to do was go home with her besties and forget about the past week. A month of pretending to be something she wasn't was going to take its toll. There was no getting away from it.

She took a step back. "That's my ride," she said.

"Come on," Juliet said, pulling out some bills and placing them on the table. "We'll see you out and we'll let him know that we mean trouble if he hurts you."

"No, you don't need to do that," Eliza said. The last thing she wanted was for her friends to try to make this right. As if she could stop them when they were determined to do whatever they wanted.

She loved her friends so much, but she didn't need them meddling with her boss. This was all pretend, fake. She and Preston weren't dating, not even close.

Still, her best friends followed her out. Preston stood by the trunk of the car, and she went to him with her bags.

"This is everything," she said.

"So, Preston, we expect you treat our girl right," Juliet said.

"What exactly are your intentions with our girl?" Mackenzie asked.

Eliza groaned. "They're doing this whole thing where they're protecting me."

"They're being your best friends," Preston said, giving her shoulder a squeeze. "I get it." He slammed the trunk down.

She wasn't going to listen to her friends' line of embarrassing questions. Climbing into the car, she stared straight ahead. "This couldn't be any more embarrassing." She thought about it, and actually, if left to her parents, this could be a whole lot worse.

Seconds passed, then minutes.

She screamed when there was a knock on the window, and of course, it was Juliet and Mackenzie.

Preston had left the keys in the ignition, so the car was already running. She pressed the button that rolled down her window.

"All done," Mackenzie said.

"I hate you guys."

They each put an arm out, and even though she was sitting, and the cuddle was slightly awkward, the love she had for her friends was absolute.

"Call us every single night if you need to. We'll always be here," Juliet said.

"I will, and you've got to call me as well. Tell me what is going on with everything and anything. I want all the details. You cannot leave anything out." Juliet kissed her cheek, then Mackenzie.

They stepped back.

Tears filled her eyes.

This was the first time in her life that she was going away from her best friends. She held her hand up and waved as Preston pulled away from the curb.

She could handle this. She was totally an adult.

Glancing out of the back of the car, she could still see them, so she lifted her hand to say bye. When she could no longer see them, she turned back to face the front. Reaching into her bag, she pulled out a tissue.

"Sorry about that. We've ... this is the first time I've been away from them."

"They are closer to you than any sister," he said.

"Yep. We kind of made a pact with each other. To always be there, to never fight, that kind of thing. It was something that started out as just a couple of schoolgirls, but it stuck. I would never be without them."

"And what about boyfriends?" he asked.

"What about them?"

"Any of you dating?"

"If I was dating, I wouldn't be pretending to be your girlfriend." She shrugged. "They come and go. Some of them are assholes and don't last long. We watch each other's backs no matter what."

"That's good. That's good."

She glanced over at Preston and actually took him in. Jeans, a white shirt, and she saw the hint of a wife-beater underneath. The suit was gone.

"This is what your parents are expecting?" she asked.

"Going back to my folks is not about impressing

them with my thousand-dollar suits."

"Is that all they cost? A thousand dollars?"

He chuckled. "Come on, Eliza, you and I both know they cost a lot more than that."

"True, true. You get your amazing PA to go collect them. Still, a suit is a suit, and if you spill red wine or even grease down anything, and they're stained and ruined just like a fifty-dollar suit."

He opened his mouth, closed it, and opened it again.

"I'm going to like this," she said.

"What?"

"Being able to speak my mind."

"Don't even start. So, let's go over some of the plans right from the top," he said.

"Are you going to quiz me?" she asked.

"How many siblings do I have?"

"Three brothers and one sister. You do love them dearly."

"I never added in the last part."

"I can improvise," she said.

"Fine. Fine. What do they do?"

"I don't know?" she asked, turning toward him.

"What?"

"Remember, we agreed that when it came to your brothers, I only know their names. Same with your sister. I don't need to know anything else."

"Right, right, of course. That's what an engaged couple would know."

She smiled.

He sounded nervous.

"How long has it truly been since you last saw your parents?"

"Not that long, okay?"

"Fine." She held her hands up in surrender.

"Maybe we should talk about something else."

"Great. Let's talk about the merger of … er…"

"Mr. Aguire?"

"Yes, him."

With the way his nerves were fried right at that moment, Eliza didn't think talking about anything work-related was a good idea.

"I think we should just enjoy the peace and quiet as we drive to your parents' place."

"It's a long drive," he said.

She reached forward and turned the radio on. A song she didn't recognize blasted out of the speakers, but it was better than silence, and better than talking with her boss about their fake engagement.

****

He hadn't told the truth.

With each mile they got closer to his parents' house, his nerves picked up. Preston had gotten the call that morning to tell him his old room was ready for the two of them. He attempted to make one last-ditch attempt to get it changed, but they told him they were forward thinkers and they didn't mind him bringing his fiancée to see them. They knew all about new love and all of that.

He and Eliza were going to have to share a bed.

Fuck.

This wasn't exactly going according to plan. Now he couldn't be sure if bringing Eliza was the best. He was sure his sister had done all of this on purpose. Would a fiancé truly not tell her about his life? About his siblings? What was too much to share? He knew everything there was to know about Trudy, Roger, Kian, and Andrew. He was close to all of them, in his way.

None of them had wanted to live the city life, only him. For the longest time, he'd always wanted to make his own way, to find the path that best suited him, while his siblings had always been happy in Westcliffe Heights. Not him.

He wanted to prove to himself that he could make it without his parents' name, and he had, to a certain extent.

"We're nearly there," Eliza said.

They'd made a couple of stops along the way to use the bathroom and to get food. For the most part, they sat in silence.

The big sign welcoming them to Westcliffe Heights made his stomach turn.

This was it. There was no turning back after this.

Eliza leaned forward. It was getting dark, and it was hot as well. He'd turned the AC up to help make things comfortable for them.

After the sign, they had to drive for a mile and a half to reach the start of town. There was a small collection of houses, recently built, and the road took them through town. Nothing had changed.

"Wow, your name is on everything," Eliza said.

Not his. Boone, his father's. The hardware store, the diner, even the pharmacy, but it helped that he'd been the one to keep it funded through the bad times.

His car was gaining attention, but he ignored it.

"Some of the people are waving," she said, glancing behind her.

"I know."

"You're not waving back?"

"I will." He followed the road out of town, turning off on the left, and began the travel toward his parents' place.

The houses got larger the further he went until he came to a stop outside one of the biggest Westcliffe Heights had to offer. His father had helped to build this one from the ground up, for his mother.

As he parked the car, his heart rate picked up.

"Okay, this is … wow," she said.

"This is my family home." He turned off the ignition. "We've got about twenty seconds before they're all here."

"Mr. Boone, I mean Preston, it's eight at night."

"So, believe me when I say they are all going to want to meet you. There's something else as well…" He couldn't bring himself to say it. She'd be pissed, no doubt about it. Staring into her blue eyes, he contemplated telling her about the bedroom arrangements, but he just knew deep down that whatever he said wasn't going to come with happiness, and before she met his parents, he wasn't going to cause an argument.

"They're coming," he said.

She had pretty eyes. Had he noticed that before?

He unbuckled his seatbelt, sliding it back and opening his door. Being the gentleman he was, he quickly rounded the car as Eliza was getting out. Taking the door in his grip, he held out his hand.

She placed hers in his, and there was that electric shock again. He didn't back away but held her hand firmly within his as the pack of hungry wolves descended upon them. There was nothing wrong. They could get through this.

His mother was the first to get to him.

Preston had no choice but to break his hold on Eliza as his mom threw herself at him.

"It's so good to finally see you. I cannot believe you insisted on driving all the way out here. We know what kind of a long drive it is. We would have come to you. Now, do I get to look at her?" Marsha asked.

He glanced toward Eliza, who stood a few steps away.

"Eliza, babe, come here."

She looked like she wanted to shake her head, telling him no. There was no way he was going to let her back out.

He thought he was going to have to order her, but she took the few tiny steps toward him, and he wrapped his arms around her shoulders.

"This is Eliza Drake, my fiancée."

"Oh, my, you are gorgeous, just as I knew you would be. Let me see the ring," Marsha said.

Trudy came rushing through after their brothers. "And me. Let me see. Let me see."

They lifted Eliza's bare hand. No engagement ring. It was in his pocket, where he'd kept it after picking the thing up.

"Oh, we had to make a stop, and Eliza is always freaking out about losing stuff. She is a bit of a klutz after all." He reached into his jeans pocket and pulled out the box. "So, I offered to keep it."

"In the very box that you bought it in? You just randomly have that lying around?" Trudy asked, arms folded.

Silence.

Shit.

They knew.

They knew he was lying to them all.

"I asked him to bring the box. Normally, he just puts it in his pocket or something like that. He told me that you guys like to have a lot of fun, and I was worried that I might lose it."

They hadn't tested it for fit. There was a chance their lies were going to blow right up in their faces.

She held her hand out, and he slowly slid the ring onto her finger. He was tempted to close his eyes while they went through this stage, not wanting to admit his fear of being caught out in the lie.

"Thank you, honey," she said.

He took her hand when he saw it was a perfect fit. Pressing a kiss to her knuckles, he winked at her.

Eliza didn't look impressed. She gave him a forced smile, and much to his surprise, he wanted her teasing, her happy. Pushing those feelings to one side, he held her hand as the introductions got underway.

His dad, Greg, pulled her in for a hug, as did Trudy. Each of his brothers got a turn, but when it came time to introduce their wives, his mother just wanted them to settle in.

"We've got time to do all the catching up later. I think we should just let them settle in, and you know, find their footing and all of that." She clicked her fingers. "Let me show you to your room."

He went to the trunk, where his dad helped to unload the bags.

As he leaned in, Eliza mouthed, "Room?"

He forced a smile to his lips. "Honey, why don't you go with Mom? She will show you everything."

Then he wouldn't have to deal with her reaction immediately.

"Sure, yes, of course," Eliza said.

Her back was ramrod straight, and as she went with his mother and Trudy, he was left alone with his dad. His brothers had already gone back inside with their wives.

"She's not who I expected," Greg said.

"Who were you expecting, Dad?"

"I don't know. Someone I see in those pictures you keep. You know, the ones on the cover of magazines."

"Ah, you mean a model?"

"Son, I'm not going to judge you, but she is your

employee. Do you think that's wise?" he asked.

He knew there was a chance that no matter who he brought with him his dad wouldn't approve.

"Dad, you haven't even met Eliza yet. Just … be around her, and you'll see, she is incredible. I'm not taking advantage of her, and neither is she with me. This feeling between us is mutual, okay? She's already feeling awkward about meeting you guys, especially knowing my reputation." He took a deep breath. The lies fell from him so fast. He needed to put a check on himself.

They carried their cases through the house, and Preston didn't need to be told where exactly they were. He went straight to his old bedroom.

This was his family's home. It wasn't like his apartment, though, with no memories, or artwork.

His parents were family people. They had memories on every single wall. Camping trips, special occasions. The odd picture that seemed to be taken just right. This was his family. His home.

Seeing all this, he didn't feel swallowed by the legacy for the first time. This was his family.

"You don't need to worry, sweetheart. I'm not too old to know what goes on between a newly engaged couple. There's no need for a second bedroom. I'm so pleased to have you both under my roof."

He entered the bedroom, and sure enough, Eliza stood there, fake smile and all.

"Honey," she said.

"I told you not to worry about the second bedroom. My parents are forward-thinking and know that relationships have…" He couldn't bring himself to say it.

"Sex?" Marsha asked.

He felt his face heating, and Eliza looked mortified.

Fortunately, his parents weren't paying attention.

"You must be hungry. We've saved you some dinner. We'll let you guys get settled, and then, we'll see you downstairs."

He watched as Trudy, his mother, then his father, each left the room. In his mind, they left like the warning bell.

Ding.

Ding.

Ding.

The door closed.

"What the hell?" Eliza asked.

"You're upset about the room, and you should totally be upset about that, because I didn't tell you that my parents had already decided that we will be sleeping in my bedroom."

"There is only one bed. What are we going to do?" she asked.

"Look, I know you're upset, but the bed is pretty big enough for the both of us. We can do this."

"I don't know. This is a whole new level of lying. Your family really cares about you, Preston. I don't think we should be doing this."

"Then do me a favor and don't actually think about what we're doing. It will make it so much easier." He turned toward her, hands on hips.

"And what is this?" she asked, holding up her hand.

"It's an engagement ring."

"It's huge, Preston. This thing is fake. Why would you get me a huge engagement ring? Are you wanting to make me look like a fool?" she asked.

He took her hand and ran his thumb across her engagement ring. "I got you a ring this big because that is what exactly I would get my fiancée, Eliza. I'm not just playing a role, I'm trying to make it work."

"You'd get your fiancée this?"

"Yes, I would." He let go of her hand. "Look, my parents are ... they're in love, okay? They have always been in love. They like to make a big deal out of everything, which is why we're sharing the room. This isn't new for them. They just try to do everything to make our lives as bearable as possible."

"I don't think I can do this," Eliza said.

He sighed and sat down on the edge of the bed. "I understand that. My parents are a little ... much."

"Are you embarrassed by them?" she asked.

"What? No, hell, no. I love my parents."

She moved to sit beside him. "I got a sense that you were pissed with your dad."

"That? It's nothing. Just the same old shit but different days." He ran a hand down his face. "The truth is, I haven't stayed back home for long, in a long time."

"Why not?"

"I don't want to talk about it."

"Okay. I get that. So we don't talk about it, ever." She got to her feet. "Fine. You know what, I can totally do this. Sharing a bed with my boss to have a job for life, totally worth it. We can do this, Preston. We can be the most amazing engaged couple, get the Aguire deal, and life will be perfect."

It was strange, but he believed her.

Chapter Eight

"We're so screwed," Eliza said, arranging her perfume bottles.

They had already gone down to eat some food, and her stomach cramped. They were too stilted. The time they'd spent together wasn't helping. Around his parents, she found herself feeling wooden. Like they would know she was lying to them. What didn't help was the constant glint of the engagement ring.

There was no denying it was a beautiful ring. Breathtaking, but the moment he slid it on her finger, her entire body had clammed up.

These were true lies they were telling his parents.

Marsha was telling her about how she wanted him to settle down. To find a nice girl to start a family with.

"Calm down," Juliet said.

"I cannot calm down. I am freaking out."

"Where are you?" Mackenzie asked.

"Our bathroom. We just had the dinner from hell, and now we've got to share a room. With one bed. One. He lied to me," she said.

"Eliza, you get to sleep in the same bed as a hot guy. Don't think of the particulars."

She groaned. "You two are not helping. You're supposed to be on my side, and it feels like you're taking his."

They both denied it.

"I don't think I can do this," Eliza said.

Her doubts had been mounting by the second. She felt sick to her stomach, not to mention the overriding fear of being a disappointment.

"You've got this," Juliet said.

"If you don't want to do this, then you can come

home, and you can look for another job. We both know if you fail at this, you won't want to stay working with him."

Eliza groaned.

The long hours.

The pain in the ass he'd been.

For the most part, she happened to love her job. There were a few elements she couldn't stand, like the destruction of other companies. Seeing Preston let people go. That was hard.

She rested her head against the mirror and groaned. "I'm not coming home. I will not admit defeat so easily."

"Just pretend like you still have a crush on him," Juliet said.

"I never had a crush on Preston Boone," she said.

There was silence over the line.

"Of course, you didn't. Why would you have a crush on your boss in the early days before you got to work for him?" Mackenzie asked. "You just talked about him a lot."

"No, no, no, no, hell, no, I did not have a crush on my boss. Is that what you think it was?"

"Oh, our pizza just arrived. We've got to go."

"No. No, you do not get to hang up on me."

But they already had.

She put her cell phone on the counter and lifted her head to stare at her reflection. "I did not have a crush. Not now. Not ever. He's my boss. There was no crush." She wasn't even going to waste the time thinking about their thoughts. It was pointless.

She'd already taken a shower, and now she ran fingers through her long blonde hair, allowing her hair to dry naturally.

She was so tired, but Preston was in the other

room.

"I can do this. I can totally do this." Nodding at her reflection, she stepped out into the room. Preston had pulled off his shirt and wore only his sweatpants.

Eliza's hands clenched into fists as she realized she wore her silk negligee and hadn't taken a robe into the bedroom.

She chose not to cover her chest and instead, to ignore him, and moved toward the bed. Staring down at the large piece of furniture, she wrinkled her nose.

"Have you … does this have … er…" This was so mortifying.

"I haven't slept with another woman in this bedroom."

"Right, okay, good, right, yes, of course. Do you, er, have a preference for where you sleep?" she asked.

"Nope. Find a spot and enjoy." He left the bedroom, and she pulled back the covers. It was warm, but not unbearable.

Sliding into bed, she noticed the mattress was so comfortable. At first, she lay on her side, which gave her the perfect angle of the door so she'd see if he came in or out.

She hated that, so she quickly rolled over and looked off toward the far wall. His bedroom didn't have any pictures, which was odd.

The whole house had so many pictures. It didn't look cluttered, but this was a close family with a lot of memories. Marsha had taken her toward the family of wedding photos. All but Trudy and Preston had a picture on there.

"I'm hoping for you all to be on there someday," Marsha said.

That was when the worry had set in.

Pretending to people she had never met, super

easy. When she finally put faces to names, well, that made her job even harder. She hated it.

This wasn't going to go well.

The door opened, and she tensed up as Preston entered the bedroom.

They were sharing a bed. This wasn't appropriate in any way, but she made sure to stay perfectly still, to not move a muscle.

"I know you're still awake," he said.

"I'm not trying to hide it."

He wore a pair of boxers and nothing else. His body was a work of art. For a man who sat behind a desk all day, he shouldn't look good at all, and yet, he did. It wasn't fair.

Eliza pulled back, but she didn't realize she was so close to the edge of the bed already, that pushing away put her precariously on the edge, and she let out a scream as she toppled out of the bed, hitting her ass on the floor.

"Are you okay?" Preston asked.

"Yeah, yeah, I'm fine. Just my dignity." She groaned.

Her negligee had ridden up, exposing more of her thighs. She wasn't going to do the comparison between their bodies. Her boss was a machine. She was starting to wonder if he was government issue, while she was everything natural.

Moving to her knees, she placed her arms on the edge of the bed and looked up at him. He'd leaned over the bed to look at her, and she forced a smile to her lips.

"You're in my spot," she said.

"Oh, right, your spot."

"You told me to pick one. This is what I picked." She was rambling. She didn't care what spot on the bed she had, just so long as she could actually sleep.

Preston moved back, giving her the space she

needed to slide into bed with as much dignity as one could muster.

Her ass was sore, and she tried to discreetly rub her ass.

"Do you want me to rub it better?" Preston asked.

She jerked her head up to look at him. He was kidding, right?

"You want to rub my ass better?"

He laughed. "I don't know. It might stop you from being so tense."

"You're finding this funny, aren't you?"

"Eliza, babe, we've got a whole month of this, and if you can't handle one night, then I don't know how we're going to handle a full day, let alone a month. My family is going to see through this."

"Why don't you tell them the truth?" she asked.

"You want to stick around while I tell them I arranged this big lie because of my sister?" he asked. "You saw the mantel of wedding ceremonies."

"Your sister isn't there."

"That's because my sister is hiding something big from my parents and she's too scared to tell them."

"What?" Eliza asked.

He opened his mouth and closed it.

"You're right. This isn't my business," she said.

"My sister is ... she is in love with a woman," he said.

"Wait, what?"

"Yep, she has been since college. She lives with her. Our parents don't know the truth because she is terrified of disappointing them. She's the only daughter and all that."

Eliza frowned. "I don't think your parents will mind."

"I know, but ask Caroline, my sister's girlfriend,

how her parents took it."

"Not well?"

"They disowned her big time. Cut her off. She had no choice but to leave town."

"Caroline's not from Westcliffe Heights?"

"Nope. Trudy brought her to Westcliffe. Told my parents some of what happened, not all of it, and well, you know what they say, the rest is history."

"Have you met Caroline?"

"Yeah, she's a sweet woman." He groaned. "Okay, seeing as you haven't run for the hills yet, then I better tell you that my parents thought I was in love with Caroline."

"They did?"

"Yeah, I'm not. I just … when it all kind of kicked off, I was around, and I helped Trudy to move Caroline in. My parents didn't get it. They thought I was helping her out because of my feelings for her, and I think they may assume the reason I've never brought a girlfriend or a fiancée back to town was because of that."

"Wow," Eliza said.

"Yeah, wow."

"Your family is amazing," Eliza said.

"What about your family?" he asked.

"My family is pretty good. I don't have any siblings. My parents wanted more kids, but there were complications while she was having me, so I was the only one. They are wonderful parents. I'm not going to claim they were anything but. They would like to see me settle down. Not living with my best friends. You know, they want the best for me. It's why they can never find out about this," she said. "If they did, our wedding would be planned for next week, and we'd have a dress, a caterer, and all that."

"Were you one of those girls that planned out

your wedding when you were a kid?" he asked.

She frowned and shook her head. "No, I wasn't. I never had a thing for horses either, in case you're wondering."

He chuckled. "What did you love then?" he asked.

"My friends. I guess I ... I don't know, being the big girls in school, we were..." She groaned. "I'm going to tell you this, but I don't want pity or you thinking anything bad, okay?"

"Yeah, sure, I'm all ears."

"Juliet, Mackenzie, and I, we were ... bullied about our weight and other things. We kind of found each other and realized there was this bond and unity between us. So long as we stuck together, nothing would ever hurt us. It is so totally lame telling you about this, but it was the way it worked for us. We were inseparable. Our folks always said that we'd grow apart. Different colleges and all that."

"You didn't grow apart, did you?"

"Nope. The same college suckers. We're the best of friends."

"I can see that. They're good people, Eliza."

"And so is your family." She stared into his eyes, seeing he was genuine.

After all the travel and the revelation of sharing his bed, it was becoming a little too much for her, and she tried to stifle her yawn, but she ended up covering her mouth.

"I'm so sorry. I don't know where that came from. I'm so tired." She started to chuckle.

"It's fine. Goodnight."

Eliza tensed up as Preston leaned over and kissed her forehead.

It wasn't an overtly sexual kiss, but it seemed the

most natural kiss in the world.

He pulled away and tensed up. "Can we just pretend I didn't do that?" he asked.

"Yes, we can pretend. In case you didn't know, I'm all about the pretend."

****

Preston felt the nicest ass he'd felt in a long time nestled against his dick.

His hand was full with a large, firm tit, more than a handful, and the vanilla scent coming from the hair close to his face was somewhat intoxicating.

Opening his eyes, he saw the blonde hair, and slowly, piece by piece, he became very much aware of who he was holding.

At the same time, Eliza gave a little wiggle, tensed up, and within seconds, they had sprung apart. Both of them on either end of the bed.

"That was—" they said at the same time and stopped right on point.

Eliza's gaze dropped down to his dick, and he quickly dropped his hands.

"You have an erection!"

"I'm a guy, okay? It's what guys get when their hands are full of a gorgeous woman." Eliza's ass and tits had been fucking glorious in his hands.

There was a sudden knock on his door, and they both turned to each other.

"Wakey. Wakey. Breakfast is nearly at the table," his mother said.

"We've just woken up. We'll be down soon," he said.

"Oh, okay, well, forgive this interruption, and you two get right back to what you two were doing."

He groaned.

Eliza's mouth fell open. "She thinks we were

having sex?"

"Yes," he said. "Why are we whispering?"

"Because we were not having sex."

"I know that. Do you want to use the bathroom?" he asked.

Her gaze fell to his crotch again, and it wasn't exactly helping. He was still very much aroused. "Yes, I think I better."

She spun away, and he couldn't help but look at her curvy ass. He had to admit he'd admired her curvy behind plenty of times in the office, but always covertly so no one would ever notice. Up close, rubbing against his dick, it was even better.

Running a hand down his face, he looked down at his dick. "Down, boy. This isn't happening."

He didn't even think Eliza liked him like that.

Focusing on the bed, he started to count numbers, and slowly, his erect cock ebbed away. By the time Eliza came out of the bathroom, wearing a robe, he was in a more comfortable position.

"All yours," she said.

He brushed past her, ignoring the pull of wanting to touch her, and went to the bathroom, where he slammed the door closed.

Pushing his boxer briefs down, he stepped into the shower and turned it on, basking in the freezing cold temperatures. This was what he needed. The hard sting of the cold. It would get him focused on the mission at hand. Eliza was a job. She was pretending to be his fiancée. Nothing more.

She was his PA.

A damn good one.

One he didn't want to lose because he couldn't keep it in his pants. He was a good boss, had a great work ethic.

Everything was going to be okay.

He refused to fuck this up.

He finished in the shower quickly, turning off the water and wrapping a towel around his waist. Then he moved toward the sink.

"You can do this," Preston said to his reflection.

This was proving to be a little more difficult than he imagined. The reality of what he'd told his sister was starting to sink in.

He'd been around engaged couples, and they were closer, in love, connected. He and Eliza looked like a boss and employee.

It didn't matter. They were going to fix this.

Leaving the bathroom, he found Eliza seated on the edge of the bed, just as he'd imagined her waiting for him.

"You're not dressed." She closed her eyes.

"No, I'm not. Don't worry. I'll be dressed in a second." He walked into the closet and found a pair of linen shorts and a shirt.

Sticking to the closet, he stripped off his towel, changed, and exited the closet. Eliza's fingers were slightly spread apart as if she didn't want to see but also couldn't help but look.

"You want to get a full frontal?" he asked.

"No. No. Of course not." She dropped her hand.

"About this morning," he said.

She held her hand up. "No, let's not go there. We are not in control of what we do while we're asleep. It happens all the time, right? People who are complete strangers end up cuddling each other and putting their hands on completely inappropriate body parts. The moment you realized you were … touching my breast and hip, you stopped. That's the main thing. We don't have to talk about anything else. I feel fine. What about you? Do you feel fine?"

She rambled, and he found it so cute.

"I'm fine. I don't want you to be uncomfortable."

Eliza snorted. "It's fine. Totally fine. Do you think we should go and get breakfast?" She was already walking ahead of him, going toward the door.

He couldn't help but smile at her.

She was so cute.

Again, his gaze dropped to her ass. She wore a pair of shorts and a tank top as well, one that seemed to cling to all of her curves. She wore a pair of flat sandals, and he couldn't help but admire her calves. He'd never been a leg person, but he loved how thick and juicy her thighs were.

Get focused.

He didn't have the time or luxury of thinking about Eliza as his. This wasn't real. What they shared wasn't real.

Shaking off his interest, he followed behind her, placing a hand at her back to guide her toward the dining room.

As to be expected, the table was full of food, and everyone who was anyone was around the table. The full spectrum of family, who all went silent and turned toward them.

Great. This was great.

His mother was the first one to come forward. She cupped Eliza's face and pretty much dragged her away.

Roger came toward him, looking smug. "I thought you said you were never going to marry."

"I never said that," he said, the lie falling easily from his lips.

"Admittedly, everyone thought it was going to be with Caroline, but this is good. Eliza seems nice."

He slapped his brother on the back. "She is." He stepped toward the table and went straight to where his woman sat. There was a singular chair available.

"Well, well, big brother, this is a surprise. Normally, you try to stay as far away from us lady folk as possible," Trudy said.

There was a chorus of laughter.

"Yeah, well, I've got to protect my woman from your evilness."

Trudy blew him a raspberry.

"Eliza, I'd like to introduce you to Lydia, she is married to my brother Roger." He pointed toward Lydia.

"So formal with all of these introductions," Lydia said.

He wasn't going to point out to her that he'd only done one so far.

"This is Grace, and she's with Kian. I have no idea why. She is way too good for him."

Grace laughed. "You charmer."

"And finally, you've got Scarlett, who for some reason, decided she was in love with the youngest one of us all, Andrew."

"It wasn't exactly hard to fall for him. He's a sweetheart and you all know it."

He did know it.

Andrew had a heart of gold. Growing up, there were often times he felt people took advantage of his brother's good nature. He didn't like it, not one bit. Andrew was the person in control of the family's charity organizations, and he helped to push for donations and organized special events in the town.

He was a well-loved guy. Everyone adored him.

"Ladies, this is my fiancée, Eliza."

"We can see that," Lydia said. "Ever since Roger told me you were engaged, I couldn't wait to meet the lucky woman who finally snagged you."

Preston couldn't help but laugh.

Lydia wasn't his biggest supporter. She felt, as he imagined many of his family did, that he'd abandoned them to go on to bigger and better things. He'd often heard her say that he felt he was better than all of them. It was never the case, but he refused to get into an argument with family over the decisions he'd made for himself. This was his life, and he'd do whatever the hell he wanted to do with it, and to hell with what other people said.

"Tell me, Eliza, what made you fall madly in love with him?" Grace asked.

Eliza's face had turned a slightly deeper shade of red. This wasn't good. They'd never discussed this element before.

"Wow, it would be easier to say what I don't love about him. I guess at first, it was the fact he gave me this incredible opportunity. I know. I know. I work for him, and there never should have been a relationship developing, and I get that. It's the little things that started it. He'd ask me to get me coffee, and he'd hand me the company card, and he'd tell me to make sure I got myself whatever I wanted. In his own way, he'd take care of me, probably without even realizing, and over time, I slowly fell in love with him."

Preston was blown away. For a short second there, he actually thought Eliza was telling the truth.

"He'd never allow any of the men or women he dealt with to treat me like crap. If they tried to abuse their position within the boardroom, or a meeting, or whatnot, he'd put his foot down. Demand that they apologize for insulting me. Little by little, he got under my skin."

"Aw, now that is a love story in the making," Grace said.

"I didn't know you had it in you, big bro," Roger said.

He chuckled. "I guess I'm good at surprising everyone."

"So when did you two, you know, even realize that you wanted to be together?" Scarlett asked.

These weren't questions he anticipated. His mother got up, asking for them to hold that thought, and came out seconds later with more pieces of bacon.

He distracted himself with filling his breakfast plate.

"Well?" Scarlett asked when a short time had passed.

"I'll let Preston answer this. It was he who made the first move," Eliza said.

All gazes turned toward him. It felt similar to the night he said he'd started up his own company and was heading to the city. How he didn't want to stay in Westcliffe Heights and had big plans of his own.

"Her ass," Preston said.

This created a few chuckles. His mom slapped him on the arm.

"No, I ... she's amazing. When I first hired her, I thought I'd made a big mistake. I didn't know anything about her. Within the space of a few days, my chaotic life had order. She made sure everything was dealt with swiftly. Day by day, month by month, I started to notice her. The first time was when she dropped a file leaving my office. She bent down, and I looked up, and I admired the curve of her ass. It was the first time I noticed her as a woman, not as my PA. From there, my feelings just built, until one day, we were waiting for an elevator, and I just felt this connection. I dropped my case, grabbed her, pressed her up against the wall, and kissed her. From that day on, we've been pretty inseparable."

Silence met his explanation.

It was a combination of truth and lies.

He did notice her ass. They had stood by an elevator several months ago when he got this overwhelming urge to kiss her.

He didn't.

The elevator arrived, the moment was lost, they got in, and the rest was history. But the desire to kiss her, really kiss her, had never gone away.

Glancing at her now, he saw that she looked a little blown away, but she quickly masked it.

Chapter Nine

She wanted to experience that kiss.

Life was so unfair.

The way Preston described it, she could actually visualize it. There had been a moment, many months ago, one she'd never told her best friends about because the truth was, she'd felt it was inside her head.

Was it the same moment near an elevator Preston was talking about?

She didn't know, and there was no way to ask him because she was suddenly being taken out to go check out the town with Marsha, Trudy, Lydia, Grace, and Scarlett. The men were staying back at the house, keeping an eye on the children.

They were not using cars to get to town either. She was pleased she had used flat shoes.

Preston had given her a cell phone and told her if she needed any help, not to hesitate calling him.

She hadn't agreed to this. He'd promised to be with her constantly.

Her stomach was in knots. The breakfast had been amazing, but she hadn't taken the time to enjoy it, seeing as she was the object of so many questions.

Marsha moved toward her side, sliding an arm through hers. "It is such a beautiful day."

"It is."

It was so hot. Not too uncomfortable, at least not yet, but she couldn't deny how beautiful the houses looked in the summer.

The glorious sunshine and snow were the two weather types that made anywhere in the world look beautiful.

"You know, I'm relieved," Marsha said.

"You are? What about?"

"You." Marsha rested her head against her shoulder. "When Trudy told us he'd gotten engaged, I imagined a gold-digger. I hated myself for thinking it. To even put a fellow woman in that category, but I bet you've seen all kinds of women in and out of his life with how long you've known him."

"I have." She wasn't going to bring up the women he'd gotten her to buy a parting gift for. All of it had been jewelry. All of it had been expensive as well. She'd never forget the time one of the women had come back with the bracelet he'd picked out for her. It had been expensive, but to the woman already dripping in gold and diamonds, it hadn't been enough.

It was the first time Eliza had hated her sex that day. She'd met a gold-digger only interested in Preston's money, not in the man himself.

"Preston has always had so many big dreams. His father and I knew from the start that he wouldn't stay in Westcliffe. He was a stubborn boy."

"Roger always said he was a main alpha. Needed to prove that he, himself, could earn enough money to support a town," Lydia said.

"That's not a bad thing," Eliza said, feeling the need to defend Preston. These women loved him as a brother, but they didn't get him. "His company helps to keep certain places afloat."

"He also destroys little companies," Scarlett said.

"It's like he found a way to be the complete opposite of his father," Grace said.

Marsha tutted.

"It's not like that," Eliza said. "Yes, he had no choice but to break apart certain companies. There are people who may lose their job because of it, but it's not due to his takeover. He tries to find the right opportunity for every single person he can. His own company employs thousands, and he gives hope to a lot of people. There are a lot of health benefits to being with him. I also know for a fact that he donates to multiple Westcliffe Heights charities."

"He does?" Marsha asked.

She nodded. Eliza knew because she'd been the one to file the checks. She knew now more than ever that Preston may have walked away from his home with the intention of building his own company, but that didn't mean for a second he'd ever truly left.

"All he's done is … expand the Boone name, and he's done it in his own way."

"You really are in love with him," Lydia said.

Marsha gave her arm a squeeze. "You're doing everything right."

"What do you mean?"

"Rushing to defend him. I can sleep happier at night knowing he's got someone watching his back."

Eliza didn't like for a second how people were judging him. It kind of pissed her off. Preston wasn't a bad guy. Sure, he was a pain-in-the-ass boss, and she'd already lied way more in the last twenty-four hours than she had in her entire life, but that didn't matter. His family loved him, she got it, but they also judged him for his life choices.

She didn't entirely know why Preston had to leave Westcliffe Heights, but without him, she wouldn't have a job, nor would anyone else.

He was an amazing man.

They walked all the way into town. Every time they met someone, Marsha gripped her arm and introduced her, adding on at the end that she was the one engaged to Preston. It wasn't long before the town would get the word out that the most eligible bachelor was now taken.

She expected more judgment from everyone, but so far, all she'd experienced was friendly faces.

They walked into town where most shops had Boone within the title.

"Preston told me his family was a big deal in town," she said.

"Greg started to earn his money at a young age. He was big into investment. What he earned from the stock market, he somehow found the way to double, then triple. He's always had a keen eye. Knew when to take his assets and when to invest. The town struggled in our early days. Where we live now, it didn't even have a house on it." Marsha smiled. "We were married young, did Preston tell you that?"

"He did."

"Yeah, Greg and I, since we were kids, knew we were always going to be together. I had no doubts, and neither did he. Our first home together was a tent on the land. He promised me before Preston was born that he'd build me a house." Marsha laughed. "My water broke as he picked me up, straining mind you, and carried me over the threshold. There is nothing that man won't do for me."

Eliza laughed. She was so happy to hear Marsha talking about her love. This was the kind of love she always wanted. Ever since she was a little girl, she wanted to be with a man who made her heart sing.

"It is rare to find that kind of strength in love," Eliza said.

"Tell me about it. Greg and I were just babies, but we knew without a shadow of a doubt. We knew we were soulmates, and no one could come between us." She sighed. "It will be a life you and Preston will have. If there is one thing I know about my son, it's that he has a soft spot in his heart for love." Marsha sighed.

"He is a good man."

They walked toward a diner, and a small, round woman came out, glaring at Marsha. "I heard the news, Marsh, why ain't I met her?"

Marsha chuckled. "Eliza, I'd like you to meet Melinda. She believes she is the town's matchmaker," Marsha said. "She is also one hell of a cook."

"Give me your palm, girly. I wants it."

Eliza frowned, not exactly wanting to give the woman her palm. Her hair was pulled back into a hairnet, and the apron she wore had a great deal of grease stains.

"Why do you want my palm?" Eliza asked.

Westcliffe was no different from her hometown. She'd grown up in a tight-knit community, where everyone knew each other and people took care of each other. If she'd been asked to give her palm back home, she would've given it, no questions asked.

The city had made her stop trusting people.

"Melinda believes she knows how long a person is going to be together. Who their mate is, and who their soul mate is. She has a gift."

"You ladies can mock me all you want, but I steered you all right, didn't I?"

"She sure did," Lydia said. "She told me Roger and I would have a rocky beginning, but it would be true love by the end, if I just followed my head. I did, and now we're happily married with three kids."

She had yet to meet all the children.

This was bad.

If Melinda's gift was in any way real, then she and Preston were screwed.

The woman held out her palm.

If she made a big deal out of this, would they suspect?

She couldn't exactly say touching strangers was

uncomfortable to her, seeing as she shook each of their hands.

Slowly, she placed her palm into Melinda's hand. The other woman had soft skin. "Ah, yes, I see. You're a little tense, honey. Meeting the Boone clan can be a real testament of strength."

This made her chuckle.

"I see. I see. You and Preston, it is so new. Too new."

Her heart started to race.

Melinda closed her eyes, running her fingers down the contours of her palm. She felt sick to her stomach of what she was going to reveal. None of this was good.

None of it.

Biting her lip, she waited.

Melinda's eyes opened and then she placed a palm against her stomach. "Your relationship will start with trouble. He or yourself will hurt each other. It will shatter an illusion, but from it, the greatest of joy will come. You will be the next one." The woman smiled. "I feel it." She nodded her head, winked at Marsha, and then went right back into the diner.

Eliza put her hand on her stomach, wanting more answers. She didn't get it. What the hell was that supposed to mean?

She went to enter the diner, but Marsha grabbed her arm. "After Melinda has made a fortune, she likes space. It's why she is the main cook."

"But, does what she say mean anything? She's not telling lies?" she asked.

Lydia, Grace, and Scarlett placed a hand on her shoulder. "Do not fear Melinda."

They took a step away from her.

Trudy stepped up toward her and hugged her

tightly. "What Melinda says does come true. People call her crazy, but everything, and I mean everything, comes to fruition. There is no way to doubt her."

Eliza looked back at the diner.

"You're afraid?" Marsha asked.

"I'm not afraid. I guess I'm just surprised. Preston and I, it is so sudden. You know. I hadn't even met his parents and we were engaged."

Marsha grabbed her hand. "And that's what makes life so thrilling. You're meeting us now, and there's no reason to fear. We're all here for you. We are all rooting for you."

Eliza smiled, but this … this was insane.

She had to talk to Melinda.

What she and Preston had was a foundation of lies. Endless lies, but none of it would lead to having a child. All Eliza saw in her future if she were to have a child with Preston was loneliness.

The kiss he'd described that morning, they'd never experienced it.

His lies were nice to hear, but that was all they were—lies.

****

"Have you thought of moving back to Westcliffe?" Roger asked as they stood outside.

Andrew and Kian were enjoying the pool, while he kept looking at his cell phone, expecting to hear from Eliza.

It was frustrating.

He hadn't expected them to be separated, but it was his family, so he should have known straight away.

"Can we not do this while I'm here?" Preston asked. "You know it only leads to arguments."

Roger sighed.

Their father was firing up the grill.

"Look, man, you're the one who thinks it leads to arguments. We all worry about you. The city life is not a good place."

"You've never been, so you can't judge."

"True, true. I guess I just miss you. It would be nice to have my big brother back. The kids miss you as well. Little Rachel doesn't even remember what you look like."

The pool was also full of kids. Roger's three, Thomas, Giles, and Rachel. Kian's daughter, Amy. Andrew's son, Terry.

They had gotten so big. It had been four years since he last saw Terry. He hadn't stayed long enough in town to get to know his family. Guilt flooded him.

He never intended to keep his distance. He loved his family. They were never a problem because he did love his family.

"I know I've been distant lately," he said. "I don't know, work and all that shit." Why was he making excuses?

"You know you can do just as much work from home. There is a place at the end of the street that has come up for sale. It is a big place. Mom and Dad would love for you to return."

Every other time, Preston would tell him to leave it be. How he had a home back in the city. They'd start arguing about how an apartment wasn't a home, only a tiny place.

"I think I might give that a look," he said.

Roger clapped his hands, laughing. "Holy shit, for real?"

"Yeah, I will."

"I'll tell Lydia. She has been complaining that this place is so freaking nice but no one will give it the time of day. I warn you, it's got a pretty steep price."

"Price isn't an issue," Preston said. "This doesn't mean I'm moving back or anything."

"No, but it means that Westcliffe is still in your veins, brother. You can deny it all you want. This is your home, and you know it too." Roger gripped his shoulder tightly. Lydia was a realtor.

It was how Roger met her. He'd been hoping to move out of his home, and Lydia had shown him all the apartments in town. One date led to another, and they'd been married within six months, and pregnant by the end of the year.

Preston went over to his father. "You need any help?"

"Never come between a man and his grill, son. You know the drill."

He laughed. "Yeah, I remember. Even when we were kids you were pretty protective of this grill."

"There is nothing wrong with wanting to protect. That's all I'm saying." His dad held his hands out.

It was a large grill. There were three separate iron grills, and the coals underneath were spread from extreme, to mild heat.

"The art in grilling is knowing when everything is cooked. You know the story of how I poisoned your mother the first time I got this grill."

Preston laughed. "Yeah, I remember. She told me she wouldn't eat a thing from you until you took a food safety course."

"The woman was right. I was cooking my chicken all wrong. Now, I know the sweet spot." He kissed the tips of his fingers and raised them in the air. "Your mother loves my grilled food."

Preston folded his arms. "You haven't said anything about Eliza."

"What do you want me to say?" Greg asked. "I

haven't gotten the chance to talk to her. From what I see, she's a nice girl, but I can't go giving you an opinion based on looks alone. She seems nice. That's all I can say."

"Dad, come on. I know you adored Lydia, Grace, and Scarlett the first time you met them."

Greg sighed. "No, Preston, I didn't love them the first time I met them. All you heard was the boys' interpretation. I reserve all of my judgments until I get to know them better. You, of all people, should know that."

"And why the hell should I know that?"

"You're a businessman, Preston. You know that you've got to keep your feelings pretty close to your chest. You can't let the world be able to read you. But I do have a question for you, son. Have you stopped being able to read yourself?"

There were moments, like now, that he hated his father. Greg Boone was a good man, but he was also the kind of man who saw everything.

Pretending with Eliza was a long shot.

His dad wasn't convinced, which was why he wasn't going to call her out.

Crap.

He should have seen this coming. Even if he'd done nothing wrong but was thinking about doing something, his father always caught him prior to the act. His dad was a goddamn machine when it came to reading them.

He had to do something with Eliza. To make them believe.

"You're firing up the grill?" Marsha asked. "I just knew you would."

His mother appeared out of thin air.

A chorus of *mommies* filled the air. The kids moving out of the pool, running to their mothers.

Preston watched, feeling a little empty inside. One day, he wanted kids. A whole fleet of them. Kids hadn't been in his future, not while he had a career to build up. A name to make for himself.

Eliza came through the door, carrying two giant grocery bags.

Roger took one, as did Kian, leaving her free and clear.

He walked toward her. Those lips called to him, and he didn't care if this broke their kissing rule, or if it pissed her off.

Sinking his fingers into her hair, he pulled her in close against him. Not caring there were children present, he finally kissed Eliza like he'd been dreaming of since that damn elevator.

He stole the kiss he'd wanted to take all of those months ago.

Her lips were soft like he imagined.

At first, Eliza was tense in his arms, her body too stiff to enjoy. One taste wasn't enough. He traced his tongue across her bottom lip and heard her gasp, opening her mouth, and he took full advantage, plunging his tongue inside.

Eliza gripped his shirt. She didn't push him away, and he felt that was an achievement all on its own. Deepening the kiss, he heard her gasp, her moan.

Someone cleared their throat.

Coming back to the present, he kissed her on the lips one more time. "I missed you," he said.

"I noticed." Her lips were swollen.

He wrapped his arm around her waist, pulling her against his side. "She hasn't been away from me in nearly three years."

Preston was also terrified of what his parents would say to her.

Trudy chuckled. "I think Melinda's premonition is going to come true."

"Melinda?" He remembered Melinda. One summer when he was sixteen, he'd worked at the diner.

Melinda had been a force to be reckoned with, but at the same time, once all the work was done, she'd been a sweet woman. She'd grabbed his hand on the last day before he was due to go back to school the next.

She'd run her fingers all over his palm and smiled.

"You will find everything you seek. You'll be your own man. Trust your instincts. Don't ever let your guard down. She will come to you. The woman of ten."

It was a strange message. He'd never told anyone about it.

"You're going to have a baby one day," Lydia said.

"She put her hand on Eliza's stomach and told her straight, you guys would have a troubled start, but a baby will bring you guys back together."

This wasn't good.

"I need to go to the bathroom," Eliza said. "I'll be back." She pulled out of his arms, and he watched her go.

"Oh, I think Melinda scared her a bit. She does want kids, doesn't she?" Grace asked.

All eyes were on him.

"Yes, of course."

"Do you still want your football team of kids?" Marsha asked.

"I'll be back in a minute." He wanted to be a dad more than anything, but kids came with sacrifices, and with the company, he hadn't been willing to compromise.

Woman of ten.

He'd never understood what that meant.

Preston went to his bedroom, finding the door shut. He tested it, but it wasn't locked.

Opening the door, he looked toward the en-suite bathroom and was surprised to find this door was locked.

Why would she lock this door?

"Eliza, it's me. Come on, open the door."

"Is it just you?"

"Of course. No one else would follow me." It was his family, so there was a high chance someone would. No one had though.

Eliza flicked the lock and opened the door. She hadn't started packing a bag, so that was a relief.

"I don't think I can do this."

"We are doing this."

"No, lying to your parents and family is one thing, but that Melinda ... what is her deal? She is a liar, right? Just someone you all pacify because she has amazing burgers?"

"She is still serving her house special?"

"I'm guessing so. I saw the sign that said the house special and dessert were on offer." She frowned, shook her head, and held up her hand. "That's beside the point. We're not talking about what Melinda had to offer in terms of food. We're talking about this." She pointed at her stomach.

"Eliza, unless you've been sleeping with someone else, we're not having a baby."

"I know I'm not pregnant, Preston. Is she crazy?"

He wanted to tell her not to worry. How people did pacify Melinda, but then he'd be lying.

"Oh, God, I see it in your face. We're going to get pregnant, and it's going to be awful. We're only going to agree to stay with each other for the child's sake. I feel sick." She sat down on the toilet, resting her head in her hands with her elbows on her knees.

This was new for him.

Eliza was always so calm and collected. Even in meetings, if they were starting to get heated, she had a way about her to calm everyone down and to bring the meeting back to a reasonable place. He'd never experienced her close to losing it.

He didn't like it.

"We're not going to get pregnant, Eliza. For that to happen, we need to have sex, and we're not doing that, remember?"

"That kiss?"

"That kiss was because my dad knows."

"He knows that we kissed?" she asked.

"No. The whole family knows we kissed, but he suspects we're lying and I don't want him to suspect anything."

"Has he told you?" Eliza asked.

"He hasn't needed to tell me. I know my dad. I know what he's capable of, and believe me, he suspects we're not an actual couple. So I had to break the kissing boundary."

"Preston, I have a feeling we're going to have to break a lot of boundaries. Your family is so nice, and they know you so well. Why couldn't you have come from a family that didn't care?" she asked.

He laughed. He couldn't help it. "I'll try to remember that the next time I'm being born."

"I'm sorry. I'm just freaking out. I've never been to a psychic before. I didn't even believe in them."

"Melinda doesn't consider herself a psychic."

"She doesn't?"

"No."

"Then why does she demand to hold someone's palm?"

"She only does it when she gets this feeling. If

she doesn't feel anything, then she doesn't ask for anyone's palm. It doesn't happen often. It is rare."

"I don't know, that seemed to freak me out," Eliza said.

"Do you not want kids?" he asked.

"Want kids? I do. I want so many of them. To have a house full of them, you know. I want to be a mom, but I want to find the right man who wants the same things I do."

"I get it," he said.

"What about you?"

"Honestly?" he asked.

She nodded.

"I want dozens of kids."

Chapter Ten

"So that's three of your ten?" Mackenzie said.

"Can we not talk about that stupid list I made all those years ago and focus on what this Melinda woman said to me? You guys are my rock. You need to pull me down from the ledge," Eliza said.

"Hate to break it to you, you've locked yourself in the bathroom while the family is getting ready for dinner. Don't you think they're going to assume you're taking a number two?" Juliet asked.

Eliza wrinkled her nose. "I said I was also changing into my swimsuit. Perfect explanation for being in my room, and I didn't say I was going to the bathroom."

No, she'd locked the main bedroom door, then the bathroom door, just so she could have a private conversation with her two best friends.

"I want to meet this Melinda," Mackenzie said.

"Me too." This came from Juliet.

"Neither of you are going to meet her because you're going to tell me that what she says is lies. I'm freaking out right now, and I need my two best friends to be logical. Not wanting to come and get your palms read." She groaned. "I'm sorry. I didn't mean it like that. You can come down, by all means. I wouldn't mind." She would have loved the company.

Mackenzie and Juliet laughed.

"Not helping," Eliza said.

"You, yourself, have said many times how you don't believe in any superstitions and yet, you're on the phone, telling us about a woman you've met once, and now you're scaring yourself about it."

"She was really scary," Eliza said. "I don't know. I think it's because the other women were so convinced what she said was real."

"What other women?"

She told them about Preston's brothers, their wives, and what happened.

Silence filled the line after she explained the dynamic to them.

"You guys still there?" she asked.

"We're still here," Juliet said.

"Why have you gone silent on me, guys?" She waited.

"Er, no reason at all. Let's face it, there's no way you and Preston are going to be sleeping together. I mean having sex. You're sharing a bed, but there is a distance between the two of you. It's not like you're wrapped around each other?"

Eliza cringed. She hadn't told them about what happened this morning. How she'd woken up to him holding her breast or the feel of him against her ass.

She was in deep trouble.

"You know what, you guys are so right about everything. I'm reading far too much into this, and I just have to focus. I better be getting ready before they think I'm taking a number two." She frowned, slapping her forehead with her palm. "I better go. Bye." She hung up the phone and blew out a breath. "Everything is going to be fine."

She stood up and removed her clothes, then changed into the swimsuit and tied a robe around her waist.

Eliza wished she had Juliet's body. This was going to be a disaster. Why did she agree to a swim? Her life was going to be over before she knew it.

"It's fine. I'm awesome. That's all I need to remember. My mom told me I was awesome. I am awesome."

After unlocking the bathroom door, she went straight to the bedroom door, opening it and coming to a stop.

Preston had his hand poised to knock.

"I tried the door, but it was locked. You were taking your time," he said.

"Er, yeah. I called Juliet and Mackenzie, you know. To tell them I was fine and all that." She pressed her lips together.

"Are you okay?" he asked.

"Yeah, of course. Why wouldn't I be? I'm perfectly fine. There's nothing wrong. I am peachy."

He frowned.

"Shall we head back down to your folks?"

"Eliza, are you okay?" he asked again.

"I am. I'm fine. I think I'm just overthinking everything, you know? I'll be fine." If she said *fine* one more time, she felt she'd explode. This wasn't how she anticipated this going. They were one day in, and already she felt tense, nervous, and ready to run for the hills.

"Let's head down."

Eliza walked beside him, aware of his palm against the base of her back. It meant nothing. His touch didn't set her on fire. That kiss did not melt her panties. They were still boss and employee.

They had this covered.

His family was at a large table on the patio. The heavy scent of meats filled the air. Marsha had thrown together some potato salad and pasta salad. She couldn't help but think the woman was a machine when it came to taking care of her family.

She knew what they wanted even before they did.

"Glad you could join us," Marsha said.

Preston held out the chair for her to sit down.

"Thank you," she said.

She kept a smile on her lips, all the while thinking they were watching their every single move. Was this how a zoo animal felt?

She hated zoos.

Preston took the seat opposite her.

"Hi, I'm Rachel. You're so pretty," a young girl said.

"Hi."

"Ah, the introductions need to be taken place," Preston said.

He got all of his nieces and nephews, and she was finally introduced to the next generation of Boones.

She smiled at all of them. They were sweet kids, and when the time came to eat, she was starving.

Eliza decided to compartmentalize what was happening. Melinda was just a fluke. Her premonition about a baby was false. She and Preston were never going to have sex. They had a working relationship, nothing more, nothing less.

She had both the potato and pasta salad, not caring about the carbs or starch. She needed food.

The food was passed around, and she noticed how the mothers each stood to prepare their child's plate. She couldn't help but watch as Lydia, Grace, and Scarlett took careful attention toward their children. Their love for their children palpable.

Once their kids were served, they took a seat and started to eat their own food.

She took a mouthful of the potato salad, along with the pasta salad, and released a little moan. They were both so good.

"You enjoy the food?" Preston asked.

She chuckled. "Is it that obvious? I needed this." Between Melinda and her best friends, she needed to stop thinking. The food was a welcome distraction.

"How are you liking Westcliffe, Eliza?" Greg asked.

"It's a wonderful place. I like it."

"Have you two set a date yet?" Lydia asked.

"Wedding preparations are the worst," Scarlett said.

"You didn't mind organizing our wedding," Andrew said, reaching across the table to touch his wife's hand.

They shared a moment, and she felt lucky enough to merely watch them.

"How is your mother handling all the preparations?" Marsha asked.

Lies. More lies.

"Er, she's not. I've decided to do it myself." She glanced at Preston.

"When do you think the wedding will be taking place?" Greg asked.

"December," they both said in unison.

She kept her gaze on Preston, surprised they said the same thing.

"Wow, you always wanted a December wedding, didn't you, Preston?" Trudy asked.

"I guess it is one of the many reasons we're so well-suited," Eliza said.

This was kind of creepy. She always wanted a wedding in winter. The hope of getting married in freshly fallen snow. It just seemed so romantic to her.

Everyone would be freezing their asses off, but she would be drunk on love and happiness.

The food slowly lost its appeal.

"Have you thought about getting married here?" Marsha asked. "We could really do this place up nice for you all. It would be so nice. None of you would want for anything." She clapped her hands and gasped. "I could help you. If you want, you could give me your parents' number and I'll talk to them about getting them out here."

Eliza panicked.

"We haven't told Eliza's parents yet," Preston said.

More gazes were on them.

"You haven't told her parents that you're engaged?" Greg asked.

This was turning into a disaster.

"Because Preston is my boss, and well, I'm his employee, my parents ... they have ... er ... standards."

"We don't want them to disapprove of me before we give them chance to get to know me," Preston said. "We have a plan to tell them, don't we, darling?"

"Yep. Totally, yes."

"Speaking of family. What are your plans for Thanksgiving?" Marsha asked. "I've already got the turkeys on order. We've arranged our schedules. Can I be putting you two on the list as well? I sure hope so, because you haven't spent Thanksgiving with us in so long." His mother pouted.

"We haven't thought that far ahead." Preston looked toward her. "What about your folks?"

"Juliet, Mackenzie, and I, we tend to, er, go to my folks for Thanksgiving. If you remember, this year, you're coming along so we can tell them our big news."

"Yes, that's exactly what we're doing. Completely planned."

They weren't going to be engaged by Thanksgiving. This was all a big mistake.

She finished her plate of food, declining any offer of seconds. The appetite she had when she sat at the table had long gone.

When the ladies got to their feet to clear away the

dishes, she did the same, following suit. Carrying the plates into the kitchen, she noticed Marsha and Scarlett were nowhere in sight.

"Those kids make so much mess. It amazes me they even eat anything," Lydia said. "I'm going to clean up the potatoes on the floor. I'll be right back."

"How are you holding up?" Grace asked.

They were rinsing the dishes before placing them in the dishwasher.

"How do you mean?"

"I know it can be a little hectic with all of us. This is a big moment for his parents, you know. Fifty years together. I hope Kian and I make it that long."

"You don't think you will?" Eliza asked.

"Oh, I do. Being with him, it's like the best ride as a kid. He is everything. I never believed in love, but he made me fall for him. Of course, seeing his parents, well, that is a whole new situation. They are like dynamite. The love between them, even after all this time. Growing up, kids, they were like two rocks. Don't you think?"

"They are really something," she said. Eliza had seen the way the two looked at each other, and it was truly an amazing sight. It was what all couples should aspire to be like.

Scarlett and Marsha chose that moment to come into the kitchen.

"We know it's too early in the planning stage, but this has been passed down to every single bride to wear on their wedding day to a Boone," Marsha said. "Scarlett still had it, and now it's time for you."

A gold bracelet with blue stones glinted at her.

It was a delicate piece of jewelry, stunning.

Eliza gasped. "I cannot have that."

"Nonsense. Every bride feels this way, and you do not have to worry about a thing. Hold out your wrist."

She tried to refuse a second and a third time, but Marsha wasn't hearing any of it.

The bracelet was slid on her wrist, the clasp locked. It was a nice fit, not too loose.

"So this is the something borrowed and something blue," Marsha said. "Welcome to the family."

****

Preston had clocked the bracelet.

He knew in his parents' mind, this made it official.

Eliza was going to be his bride.

He was fucked.

If his parents found Eliza's parents, then there was no stopping what they would do. This was fast turning into one giant mess, and it wasn't supposed to be.

Sitting on the edge of the deck chair, he watched as Eliza laughed at something his mother said. She kept glancing at the pool.

He sipped at his beer and couldn't look away.

His mother pointed at the pool.

Eliza nodded, stood, and he watched as she removed the robe, revealing her body to him.

The swimsuit she wore wasn't revealing in the slightest, but it covered her body to perfection. He felt a stirring in his dick at the sight of her in the one-piece, and he wanted her. Some women didn't like to have the additional pounds, but Eliza, she looked all woman to him.

He didn't mind how her legs were together, no gap between, the roundness of her hips and stomach. He certainly wasn't going to complain about her large, heavy tits.

His mouth watered as she walked into the water, giving him a clear view of her ass.

There was no way he could sit and watch. He

took another long drink of his beer, and before he embarrassed himself, he stood and took a dive into the water, breaking the surface with ease.

He kept his eye on Eliza as she swam a few laps before resting near the edge of the pool, watching them.

Preston swam toward her.

"Are you okay?" he asked.

"Everyone keeps asking me that. Do you want to know the true answer?"

"Yes."

"Kind of freaking out. I've got that bracelet that just makes this even more real." She blew out a breath. "I don't know. I feel ... bad."

"I get it."

"Don't you?"

"We've got another three weeks and six days to get through."

Eliza groaned.

He laughed. "Don't worry. There will be times it's just us, okay. No family. No acting. How about tomorrow I take you out someplace?"

"Someplace that doesn't involve getting your palm read?"

"Yeah. Someplace where there is no one to talk to us, or see us."

"Sounds like heaven. They cannot ever talk to my mother. She would be down here planning our wedding. We'd have to go through with the entire thing as well. She'd be a nightmare, no doubt."

He glanced toward his parents. "You think they'd be any different?"

"I don't know. They love you though. Care about you a lot."

"Do they?" he asked.

She tilted her head to the side, and he caught his

parents watching them.

Preston thought about his dad and moved in a little closer.

"What are you doing?"

"We're a madly in love engaged couple. We haven't seen each other for most of the day. I'm doing what any insanely jealous fiancé would do."

"And what is that?" she asked.

He wrapped his arm around her waist, drawing her close. "Making it real. Put your arms around my neck."

She shook a little as she wrapped them around his neck. "There are kids present."

"And we are present, who don't care about public displays of affection," he said.

"This wasn't part of the agreement." Her gaze fell to his lips. "We're breaking so many rules."

"Some rules are made to be broken. We simply didn't think of the logistics," he said.

"And what are those?"

"In my parents' eyes, we spend all of our spare time pretending we're not madly in love. We play the role for the people at work. The one chance we get to be away from them, and we're not taking the opportunity. Kind of looks fake, right?"

"That's what I am, Preston. I'm your fake fiancée."

"But let's make it believable."

He didn't know if he was doing this for his parents or for himself. Sinking his fingers into her hair, he brought her lips to his and kissed her.

Once again, he felt that electric current rushing through his whole body from one kiss alone. Closing his eyes, he traced her lips, and like last time, she opened.

At some point throughout the kiss, Eliza wrapped

her legs around him, and he moved both hands to cup her voluptuous ass.

She was more than a handful.

He wanted her so badly.

His cock hardened, and all of a sudden, Eliza broke the kiss. He was pressed right against her pussy. She'd be able to feel just how hard he was.

Her gaze was wide.

"That's enough R-rated stuff in front of my kids," Roger said.

Preston smiled.

He grabbed Eliza's hand and lifted it out of the water. "This good enough for you?"

"Perfect. Let's keep it straight and narrow."

He laughed, even though he felt no humor. Kissing Eliza was an addiction. His lips tingled, and he wanted to kiss her again.

They stayed in the pool for a good hour before his brothers and sisters-in-law decided it was time for the kids to go to bed.

Eliza left the pool first, wrapping her gorgeous body in a robe and making her excuses to leave. Preston followed ten minutes later, arriving in the bedroom to find the bathroom already occupied.

He sat on the edge of the bed, waiting his turn. He'd already removed his swim trunks and had a towel wrapped around his waist, but his cock was getting harder by the second.

When Eliza appeared in the doorway of the bathroom in only a towel, he had a sudden urge to tear it off her body.

He didn't.

"I wasn't expecting you."

"I'm tired," he said.

"Me too."

She stepped away from the bathroom.

Preston wanted to find another reason to stay, to linger, to talk to her. Instead, he entered the bathroom. He didn't bother to close the door.

After dropping the towel, he threw it into the laundry basket. Stepping into the cold shower, he welcomed the sting as it hit his flesh.

It did nothing for his raging erection.

He closed his eyes, determined to rid the memory of Eliza's body from his mind.

It didn't work.

All he saw was her full body. The ripeness of her in his arms. The fullness of her ass as she filled his palms.

He ached for her. Wrapping his fingers around the length of his dick, he squeezed tightly, but nothing stopped his need.

Preston worked up and down his length, going from the base up to the tip, then back down again. He kept his movements up, imagining Eliza in front of him, on her knees, begging to take his cock.

Those lips would look so good wrapped around his length.

He increased his movements, feeling the spiraling need build. His thoughts went to the woman. Thinking of her in his bed, her legs spread, wanting him, begging him again.

Just the thought of her tight, hot pussy was enough to make him come. He spilled his seed down the drain.

Eliza Drake had gotten under his skin.

The shower had already warmed up by the time he was finished. He washed his body, and still, there was a hint of arousal. There was nothing he could do to stop it. Wrapping another towel around his waist, he entered the bedroom and found Eliza already curled up in bed.

"I'll give you some privacy." She closed her eyes.

Did she feel it?

Did she want him the way he wanted her?

The words didn't come.

This was an agreement to them. They were acting a role. Nothing was different.

He changed into a pair of boxers. Back home, he'd often sleep naked. He didn't like anything tight around his body.

Preston moved to the bed and slid beneath the covers.

"Thank you for today," he said.

"It has been a pretty tough day. I don't like lying to them. You've got a cool family, Preston."

He rolled over to find Eliza had already done so and was looking at him. He lifted his arm and rested his head against his palm. "You like them?"

"Yeah, what's not to like? They love you, you know."

"I don't know."

She frowned. "What don't you know?" she asked.

"I have to wonder half of the time if I'm a disappointment. Rather than stay and help build all of this, or at least maintain it, I went off and did my own thing. I've always wanted to do my own thing, even when I was a kid."

"You think they don't like you because of it?"

He shrugged. "I don't know. I know they love me. Love and like are two different things."

"True, but I don't think they don't like you. I believe they love you very much and they're worried about you. Families do that a lot. They worry about you."

"Do your parents?"

"All the time. They hate me being in the city. It

was our dream, though. It probably sounds stupid, but we were going to go and gain all of this experience and open up our own business. We'd create an opportunity in this world for the bigger woman."

"Bigger woman?"

"I don't think it has escaped your notice that we've all got some meat on our bones. It was what bound us together. We protected each other."

"You want to start your own business."

"We do, one day, when we're ready. I don't know if our dreams have changed a whole lot since then. My parents believe in me, but they're scared of me getting my heart broken."

"You miss them?"

"Yeah, I do. Do you miss this place and your folks when you're in the city?"

He blew out a breath. This had to be the single most honest conversation he'd ever had. "Truthfully, when I'm working, I don't miss a damn thing. It's my company, my accomplishment. Where people said I wouldn't get to do it, I defied the odds, and I did it, you know. This is all mine, and no one can take it away from me."

"But?" she asked.

"There's no *but*."

"There so is a *but*, Preston. Tell me. We've crossed so many lines today. The least we can do is be honest with each other, if we can't be honest out there."

"Now that you say it like that, being here, I don't miss city life. I don't miss the early mornings or the office banter. I don't miss the meetings, or my damn apartment." He snorted. "I sometimes think I go to work just so I'm not so fucking alone." He'd said too much.

"I know this isn't going to come as any great surprise to you, you're the boss. You can decide where you want to live." She placed a hand on his arm. "It's time for you to make the decisions that will determine your happiness. What do you want out of life, Preston?"

She removed her hand and covered her mouth. "I'm so tired."

"Get some sleep."

"Do you think you can keep your hands to yourself tonight?" she asked. "Do we need to put up a wall of pillows?"

"I can't help it if I'm a cuddler," he said.

Eliza tensed. "What did you say?"

"I'm a cuddler." He pressed a finger to his lips. "Don't tell anyone."

"Are you joking with me right now?"

"Nope. I do like to cuddle. I don't do it with just anyone," he said.

Eliza frowned at him. "You are a mystery, Preston Boone." She rolled away from him.

He wanted to reach out and touch her, but he didn't. His cock was already rock-hard, and it would be keeping him company for the next few weeks.

Chapter Eleven

Some guys liked to cuddle.

It was no big deal.

So what if being able to love snuggling and cuddling was on her list of ten things for the perfect guy. That meant nothing.

Eliza followed behind Preston, pleased his family had other plans that day. They'd woken up in another precarious position.

Preston's body flush against her. One hand on her hip, the other cupping her tit again. She'd woken just before him, instantly aware of her body. She'd had boyfriends in the past. Not the kind of boyfriend that stayed the night. She'd never shared a bed with a man for many hours.

Sleeping was such a private and personal thing. The truth was, she didn't know if she farted throughout the night. It was a crazy fear to have. Who cared if they released gas at night? She imagined most people did, but the thought of a guy being put off by that, well, it kept her away from spending the night.

Two nights.

She'd broken her rules.

He hadn't said if she did … and it was too embarrassing for her to even ask.

This was crazy.

This was her parents' fault. One morning, when she was seventeen, she'd woken up to an argument. Her dad had farted throughout the night, and her mother had been awake, and offended. At which point for the next hour over breakfast, they traded insults, which ended with them making up.

Gross.

A phobia was born that day.

Of course, she was also trying to distract herself from the fact Preston had kissed her twice. During both kisses, she'd become highly aroused, and this morning, she'd felt her pussy grow slick.

The temptation to rub her ass against his cock was so strong.

Three times, she'd felt Preston's cock.

He wasn't small.

No, he was big.

Bigger than she thought possible.

He's your boss.

This is all fake.

You are never going to have sex with him.

Sex comes with the risk of getting pregnant. Remember Melinda's premonition.

Preston had woken up before she wriggled. This time, they hadn't freaked out. He'd apologized, removed his hand, and they'd pretended like it didn't happen.

He was the first man to snuggle with her. She didn't know why she'd put it on her ten list when she had such a fear of breaking wind throughout the night.

She was crazy.

This was insane.

"Not too far," Preston said.

After another family breakfast, his parents had said they were heading out of town for a couple of days, to pick a few things up. His brothers and their wives had a few events they wanted to take the kids to, leaving her and Preston alone.

They had not stayed inside the house though because their acting needed to still be in top performance as Trudy had declared she was staying.

She and Preston still had to play the part of a devoted couple.

It was after Trudy announced she was staying that

Preston told her they were heading out on a trek.

This had started at the back of the house, heading into the woods.

"You're not going to murder me, are you?" Eliza asked, stepping over a fallen thin tree.

"Why would I do that? I can pay someone to do it for me."

"Comforting thought."

"We don't have much further to go."

"So let me get this straight, you would rather go walking in the woods than stay at home with your sister. Why?"

"In case you didn't notice, my sister does not believe in personal boundaries. With no family there, she'd ask all kinds of questions, and I'm not willing to talk to her about any of it."

"Like what?"

"She'd ask for more info on you, on us, and seeing as we're kind of winging this at the moment, I didn't think you'd appreciate me adding more craziness to the list. Also, it looked to me like you wanted to get out of the house."

"All sound arguments, and I will say, all correct," she said. "Not that your parents' house isn't great. It is. You know it is."

He laughed. "Everyone loves the place."

"Have you taken girlfriends there before? More fake fiancées coming out of the woodwork?"

"Nope, just you, baby," he said. He grabbed her hand as she was about to fall. "Mind your step. We don't want you to hurt yourself."

"Are you going to tell me again where we're going?" she asked.

"It's my secret hideout," he said.

"A secret hideout?"

"Yep."

"Preston Boone, are you telling me you were a nerd?"

He snorted. "No, I was a kid, with way too many brothers and an annoying sister. Dad knew I needed my space, and it was our bonding time. We built a fort."

"A fort?"

"You'll see." He kept hold of her hand, and she had no problem with that.

They walked for another five minutes, and then she saw the sign. *Boone's Fort.*

"Okay, this is straight out of a horror movie."

"Stop it. There's nothing scary about any of this." They walked past the tree.

"Your parents own this land?"

"Yeah, there was a big fight to buy the land. The intention was to chop down the trees, but then the land would be exposed, and the chance of a big corporation picking it up and building a mall or some other venue was too high of a risk. Dad was worried about what it would do to the town, so he bought the land. There are people who keep an eye on it for wildlife purposes, but for the most part, it's my parents' land."

Eliza winced. "By big corporations buying up land similar to this one to build for tourist reasons. Ring a bell?"

She didn't want to make the comparisons, but it was Preston who had started it.

Preston stopped and turned toward her. "You're talking about Aguire?"

"Kind of."

"It's not the same."

"How is it different?" she asked.

"It just is. His land doesn't have a whole heap of wildlife and isn't backed onto a housing estate. This is a special piece of land."

She pressed her lips together. "You're right."

He was being picky, and they both knew it. The land Aguire had, in its own way, would at some point interfere with the integrity of the town.

"Some places need to have advancement in life. It is the only way they can move forward. I know what I'm doing."

"You're right. You know what you're doing. I'm sorry. Show me your fort."

This was clearly a sore subject with Preston. He purchased many companies, tore them down, and built them back up. The Aguire project was different. Very different. This would be the first time he purchased land with the hope of building an investment opportunity like a mall or something similar.

She looked past his shoulder and gasped.

"This is the fort your dad built?"

"With our bare hands."

"You and your father built this?"

"Yep. It took us a whole summer. I take it you're impressed."

There were at least three tree houses, along with ropes to climb up into each one. Across each long trunk, they'd built bridges for him to get to each one. His father had thought of everything.

This was the place he'd come to in order to think. He'd planned his future in this very fort.

"This is incredible." She moved toward one rung of steps. "May I?"

"Be my guest."

She grabbed the rope and began to haul herself up into the first tree house. He followed up behind her, and she took a seat.

"Is it stable?"

"It hasn't fallen down yet. My dad said it would always be available for when I have kids."

She sat down, her gaze roaming around his space. She had a quick glance at his bookshelves. There were some business course management books, as well as comics. "The boy became the man?"

"Yeah. I guess he did."

She reached toward the shelf and grabbed the business management book. "Where did you get this?"

"The library."

"Were you a rebel and stole it?"

He laughed. "Nah, nothing quite so sinister. They had a sale and wanted to make room for new books. I got it cheap. A couple of dollars."

Eliza flicked through the pages. "This was where it all began, huh?"

"Yeah, it did."

"Are you proud of what you accomplished?" she asked.

"Most of the time."

"My, my, does the ultimate rich bachelor have doubts about this own company?"

He chuckled. "No doubts about my company. Just a couple of other things."

"Such as?"

"Life, I guess."

"Life?"

"Yeah, being back home, it makes me realize all that I've sacrificed, you know? This is my first time back, and I mean really back. Normally, if I was here for a couple of days, I'd be locked up in my dad's office, answering emails. Still conducting meetings." He shrugged.

"You check your emails every single morning."

"True. This is different though. This is getting

away from all of that."

"You're thinking about building a family?" she asked.

"I'm considering it." He watched her to see her reaction. Nothing. "Does this make you think of back home?"

"Sometimes. It's a small town, exactly where I come from. I don't know." She smiled.

"What is it?" he asked.

"I've yet to find the right guy to settle down with."

"You mean the right guy hasn't come along."

"Nope." She shrugged. "You never know what happens."

He couldn't help but glance down at her stomach, Melinda's premonition ringing in his head. He didn't hear the cook make it, but Eliza had recited it word for word to him. Melinda never got anything wrong.

Eliza smiled. "I bet you used to bring all of the girls to this place."

"No. You're the only one who has ever been allowed here."

"Really?"

"Really," he said.

"This place is a great make-out zone." She held her hands out as if he was slightly dumb.

"I know how good it can be, believe me, but this wasn't about luring girls here to make out with. I planned my future here." He got to his feet. "Come on, I'll take you through the tour."

He pulled open the door on the right, and Eliza laughed when she saw the bridge. "Oh, my God, this is amazing. How could you have ever left this place?"

Preston walked her toward the other tree house. "This was where I'd keep snacks." He opened a couple of boxes. "It has been years, so everything is now gone."

She chuckled. "I would expect so. I still can't believe you ever want to leave this place. I mean, seriously, Preston, this is amazing."

"Do you have a treehouse back home?"

"Nah, I wasn't the treehouse kind of person. My dad wasn't that creative. Not like your dad."

"Do you like my parents?"

"They're great people. You're lucky, Preston. I know you sometimes don't think it, but they do love you, and they support you."

He nodded. "The tour doesn't stop there." This time, Preston grabbed her hand and walked her across the next bridge. He opened the door, and sure enough, there was his furniture. Still in great condition for the most part. His dad had purchased him some secondhand beanbags to sit on. They weren't the most comfortable, but he didn't care.

Eliza laughed.

As she did, a roll of thunder struck through the air.

"It's okay," Preston said. "This place is kind of water-tight."

Eliza nodded. They took a seat on each beanbag. He wasn't going to lie, they kind of had a stink to them.

A very rotten stink.

Another crack of thunder rumbled through the sky, a flash of lightning, and then out of the blue, it started to rain.

Slowly at first, and Preston was super impressed nothing got through the roof. Then the heavens opened up and went from plain old raining to pouring it down, and the once water-tight treehouse was no more.

Eliza released a little scream.

"Crap. We've got to get to shelter."

He opened the other door and started to climb down. At the bottom, he waited for Eliza. When he was able, he grabbed her around the waist and helped her to her feet. Taking hold of her hand, he locked their fingers together, and they started to run, heading through the woods.

The large trees offered them some cover.

Eliza cried out as another crack of lightning filled the air. Seconds passed before the thunder hit, but he didn't stop.

He ran, making it close to the family's summerhouse.

Twisting the lock, he found it was already open. He moved Eliza inside first and closed the door.

They were both soaked and freezing.

"I'm going to need your clothes."

Chapter Twelve

Eliza had always wanted a treehouse. As a kid, she'd beg her dad to build her one, but he never found the time. It was only when she'd grown up that she realized why her father would never build her one.

He couldn't do it.

Her father was the least crafty, unable to do anything that came to building or decorating. Her mother often did most of the repairs around the house. It was their relationship, and she knew her mother liked it like that.

Preston's treehouses were amazing. No doubt about it.

As a kid, she would have spent so much time in one as she loved to get out of the house. Now she was soaking wet. The coolest she'd been in the past couple of weeks. The heat had been a pain in the ass, even going back to the city.

"What?" she asked.

Preston had his hand out, as if to take her clothes from her.

She couldn't help crossing her arms over her chest.

"I need your clothes. You can't wear them. They are soaked."

"It's a little warm."

"Eliza, it's freezing." He pulled his shirt off his chest. "See, I'm going to get down to my boxer briefs."

"You're going to see."

"I saw you in a swimsuit. What do you think is going to be more revealing?"

"Duh, my underwear." She wore lace. The kind of sexy lace that showed off rather than covered up.

"We're adults here, Eliza. You can trust me. I'm

not going to attack you."

"I didn't say you were." She gritted her teeth. "Fine. Fine." It was logical for her to remove her clothes in front of her boss.

She started with the buttons of her shirt, handing it to him as soon as she'd taken it off her body. Next, she wriggled out of her jeans until she stood in front of him in her matching lace bra and panties.

Folding her arms across her chest and crossing her legs, she tried to be natural. "Happy now?"

His gaze was on her body, and she raised a brow.

"I'll, er, go and throw these into the dryer," he said.

He turned on his heel, and seeing as he'd looked at her body, she was going to admire the fine shape of his ass.

Life was so unfair.

Preston had a really nice ass. It was nicely proportioned, and he was tanned as well. She wondered if he spent his downtime working out and sunbathing with equal measure.

She followed him through the sun house. She couldn't help but notice it was a pretty decent size. Actually bigger than the apartment she shared with Juliet and Mackenzie.

"This place is good too," she said. "Your family knows how to do style."

He laughed. "My mom is the miracle worker around here. She's the one that handles it all."

She nodded. They moved past the kitchen, into a separate laundry room. "Are you sure this is a sun house? Or whatever you called it?"

"It did belong to Andrew just before he moved out. Mom and Dad knew he wanted some privacy, so they converted this place into an apartment style of living. It has heating. It's a pretty cozy place."

He went to the dryer. After putting their clothes inside, he flicked the switch. "It doesn't work."

Eliza moved toward the machine and noticed it was pulled forward a little more than the other machines.

She reached behind and saw the reason. The plug had been removed. "It's out of commission. I'm guessing your parents didn't get around to replacing it."

"Crap."

"It's fine, Preston. We're just going to have to let them air dry." She reached into the dryer and started to lay their clothes out, hanging them from surfaces.

"It's going to take a long time."

"Well, I don't think my boss is going to mind. He has me on this forced vacation," Eliza said.

Preston laughed. "Good point. So, we're here." He pursed his lips. "What should we do?"

"I don't know, you tell me."

She followed him again as he moved into the kitchen. He rummaged through the cupboards and came back with a bottle of whiskey.

"Can I interest the lady in a shot to warm up?"

She snorted. "It is still a little warm."

She wasn't going to admit that the rain had chilled her a little. During the process of drying their clothes, she had forgotten about her underwear state. She quickly tried to cover her body.

"It's fine, Eliza," he said. "You don't have to be uncomfortable around me." He turned his back to her and grabbed a couple of shot glasses. "But I've got a miracle cure of all things."

He moved toward the living room.

"How come there are no sheets on the furniture?" she asked.

"My brothers come here from time to time, and

Trudy. When they need to get away with family. My parents have the kids, and this is like the love nest."

"Do I need to be careful of everything I touch?" She didn't want to be touching something that had seen other people's ... things rubbing all over it.

Preston chuckled. "Nah, my parents hire cleaners to come in and pretty much fumigate the entire place."

"Oh, that's good. So good. Have you ever used this place?"

"I've got an apartment back in the city. I don't need to be bringing any woman around here for my parents to ask questions."

"Good point." She went to perch on the edge of the chair but couldn't do it. In the end, she sat on the floor.

Preston was still laughing when he came to join her. He handed her a shot, already downing his own.

She hated whiskey. Sipping at the dark amber liquid, she struggled to contain her shudder. "So gross."

"It's all we have."

"Not tequila people, then."

"Nah, whiskey is the poison of the day."

Preston was already pouring himself a second shot as she sipped at her first. "I shouldn't do this," she said.

"What? Hang out semi-naked with your boss?" he asked.

"Drink. Last time I did this, I ended up fake engaged to my boss. It was a rather hazy time."

"Well, your boss appreciates the company." He lifted his shot and downed it.

"Okay, are you even tasting it now?"

"It's easier and doesn't burn as much if you down it in one go."

"You're lying."

"Am I?"

He raised a brow, and she hated how easy he made that look. She only ever lifted two brows. It had to be some kind of gift or something.

She knocked back her whiskey, drank it in one, and then gasped. "You lied. It burns. Holy crap, that shit is horrible."

Preston chuckled. "But it was easier to drink. Want a second?"

It was on the tip of her tongue to say no, but as if in answer, a roll of thunder filled the air. "Hell, yeah."

"You're going to be a rebel on me."

"I'm going to be whatever I need to be." She let him pour the whiskey, and this time, she didn't wait around, she downed it in one go and shook her head. "Nope. Nope. Hell, no. This is a sipping whiskey."

"Feeling warmed up?" he asked.

"Yep." And if she was honest, a little less conscious of her nakedness. "So, Preston, have you ever thought about actually finding a woman to settle down with?"

"Not found one I wanted to be with."

"You know I noticed, right?"

"Noticed what?"

She smiled. "Fill her up."

Preston poured her another shot. This time, she sipped at it. "That you don't go on as many dates with women."

"Right."

"You think I'm lying, but I'm not. When I first started working for you three years ago, nearly every month I had to go and find a new gift. Always something disgustingly expensive, and do you remember the note you'd make me write?" she asked.

"I had a good time. Thank you."

"Yeah, that was the one. Kira, the lady at the jewelry store, took pity on me. She started to set pieces aside to help me out."

He snorted. "It wasn't that bad."

"I did wonder if you were addicted to sex."

"Eliza, what makes you think I bedded all of those women?" he asked.

Had he gotten closer?

"Why buy them jewelry if you hadn't?"

"Good point. I was also buying jewelry because I'd hurt their feelings. I went on a lot of dates, but that doesn't mean I screwed them all. My parents didn't raise a playboy."

"But all those rumors about you circling the net?" she asked. Did his lips look a little more tempting in the cold light of day?

"They're just rumors. Hasn't anyone ever talked to you about fake news?"

She finished her shot, and Preston poured her another.

The space between them had seemed to close.

"I know of fake news."

"Then you should know I don't fuck every single woman I meet."

That shouldn't have made her pussy pulse, but it did. Eliza realized it had been a long time since she'd been with a man. Working for Preston Boone didn't leave much of a social life, and she'd been more interested in spending the spare time she did have with her besties than a boyfriend.

Eliza moved to her knees.

"What are you doing?" Preston asked.

Even as she screamed in her mind to stop, she somehow kept on going, moving over him to straddle his waist. He didn't push her away.

She cupped his face. "Something I know I'm going to regret."

Eliza knew she shouldn't do this. The drink was making her forget who she was, who Preston was.

She pressed her lips to his. At first, it was a slow kiss. Just a meeting of lips. Eliza liked the electric current rushing through her body. She felt on fire.

When Preston made no move to touch her, she lifted up, but then he touched her ass. Both of his hands gripped her flesh, and she kissed him deeper.

They both moaned.

Preston didn't just put his hands on her ass, he gripped each cheek tightly, massaging her with his palms. She couldn't help but cry out from the sheer pleasure of his touch. This man knew what he was doing, even as she wanted to scream at herself to stop.

He was her boss. Their engagement was all fake. But she kept on kissing him as his hands traveled up her back, going toward the back of her bra. He flicked the catch, and she let out a little moan, especially as she broke the kiss, leaning back.

Slowly, so achingly slowly, he started to lower the bra.

Just as he was about to reveal her tits, the door opened. Eliza released a scream, and Preston moved her quickly so he covered her with his body.

They both turned in time to see Trudy and another woman, laughing.

"Crap," Trudy said.

"Hey, Trudy. Hey, Caroline," Preston said.

Their moment had been interrupted, but Eliza didn't know if she was happy about it.

****

His parents arrived home early.

As did his brothers and their wives. Everyone

came back to the house, and along with it, the knowledge that he was so close to getting Eliza naked.

He didn't have a problem with her moving to straddle his lap, or feeling her against him. He'd asked her what she was doing to make sure she was in touch with her senses, nothing more, nothing less.

He didn't want to make any kind of mistakes when it came to her.

Eliza had been sound of mind. She'd wanted to kiss him.

Only, the past couple of days since their moment alone, she'd been avoiding him, big time.

Each night, she'd fall asleep, and she had started to put a wall of pillows between them. Not that it stopped him. Not in the slightest. He woke up with the pillows out of his way, his hands full of all woman, and he wasn't about to complain because he loved it, a lot. He liked having Eliza in his bed.

His family adored her, and the more time he spent with her and they saw her, they slowly fell for her.

His mother had already told him that she agreed with his choice of woman, and that shouldn't have meant anything to him, but it did.

Eliza fit into his world.

Preston had tried to talk to her about what happened in the sun house, and he'd been thwarted at every turn. Today, they'd been at his folks for nearly a week, and he'd decided to make the journey into town to go see his old boss, Melinda.

Several people from the town stopped him to talk, to congratulate. He took their praises, offered a smile, but moved on quickly.

Arriving at the diner, he went up to the main counter, and sure enough, Melinda stepped out from behind the kitchen.

"Well, well, well, I knew the day would come when a big hotshot businessman would return to me."

"Hey, Melinda," he said.

She folded her arms. "How come you're not wearing a suit?"

"I'm here to be with family. No suit required."

"Well, I'm not impressed. You know how I feel about a man in a uniform."

He couldn't help but laugh. "Fine. Next time, I'll wear a suit just for you."

"It would be greatly appreciated."

He'd missed this woman. "Do I get a hug?"

She was already rounding the counter and embracing him. "You don't have enough meat on your bones. I thought your lady friend was going to start plumping you up."

"Are you planning to cook me?" he asked. Melinda always complained that he was too skinny.

"Never. I want to see you well taken care of. Come. Come. You can work with me." His hand was grabbed, and before he knew it, he had an apron on and was already chopping up some onions for her.

She had done this to him back in the day. Melinda had told him the best way to run a business was to start in hot water, to learn how to get himself out of the pot. Most of what he knew about cooking, he'd learned from Melinda.

His mother had tried to teach him to cook, but he'd been so bored throughout the whole process. With Melinda, it was different. She didn't linger for a family dinner. Her food was incredible, and she had to be fast. Cooking at the diner was about speed and efficiency.

"I met your lady friend," Melinda said.

"Eliza."

"She's nice."

"She is."

"You put a baby inside her?"

"You said the woman I was to be with was the woman of ten," he said.

"That's what your palm read."

"What does it mean?" he asked.

"I cannot tell you the reasons why or what for. I can only tell you what I see. Talk to Eliza. She will know of the ten."

Preston wiped his hands on a towel. "Will you read it again?" he asked.

She sighed. "Nothing will change."

"Please, for me. I'm … I'm kind of in a bind right now, and I just, I need to know if there is any light."

She tutted. "You know I can't resist your charm. You and I both know you don't believe I have a gift, but I'm starting to wonder if you're asking for a second reading." She wiped her hands, grabbed his palm, and lifted it.

Melinda, much like she did all those years ago, touched his hand and closed her eyes. "You have such indecision. Being back home is a problem for you. You feel a connection to this place even when you don't want to."

He didn't believe in mediums, or people's ability to see into the future, but with Melinda, it always freaked him out. All he could gather about her was how she was able to read people. To see what others tried to hide.

She closed his hand into a fist. "You have a great fight on your hand. It's internal." She reached out to touch his head. "All in here, but if you don't get your act together and make a decision, Eliza's fate has changed." She took a step back.

"What do you mean her fate has changed? You said to me when I was sixteen that no one's fate can change once you say something, that it must come true."

"You also believed I was high from smoking weed, which I have never done." She tutted. "Do not ask for me to see if you don't like what you hear."

"If her fate changes, for the good, or for the worse?" he asked.

"I cannot answer you as to the way life falls, young man. No one has ever defied my reading, but … I was once warned of this many years ago, by my grandmother. She had the gift. She foretold of your parents' love. Of their ability to bring this town back from ruin, and they did exactly that. She told me that if anyone's fate has been changed or altered, if the true course has been removed, only misery will follow. The decision you make will determine if Eliza is happy or lives a life in constant agony."

"So no pressure then."

Melinda smiled and moved back toward him, placing her palm over his heart. "The problem with you, dear boy, is you spend way too much time thinking about everything and not doing what your heart desires. You need to stop thinking and start feeling. That is the guide you have to follow. You know what you want when it comes to Eliza, to home, to everything. Follow it."

He couldn't help but take a step back, a little shocked by the sheer power of her voice.

"Now you may go. I've done what has been needed."

When Melinda told you to leave, you left, no questions asked.

Removing his apron, he left the diner. He looked around the town, seeing the name *Boone* everywhere. As a kid, he'd sometimes get a little uncomfortable. It was a legacy he didn't feel like he could follow. This wasn't his town.

It was his father's.

Now, as a forty-year-old man, with a business of his own, a name made for himself, he felt pride at what he'd been able to achieve.

He walked home, taking his time, thinking about what all Melinda had said. Even as he wanted to think it was all lies to manipulate, he knew it wasn't. Melinda wasn't like that. Never had been.

Running a hand down his face, he tried to clear his thoughts, but all he kept thinking about was Eliza. Feeling her against him.

He ... wanted her.

He'd been wanting her for a long time, and if he stopped thinking like her boss, and just as a man, then he knew exactly what the next step was.

Arriving back home, he went toward the pool, then to the kitchen. He found his parents snuggled up on the sofa, kissing. Gross. "Have you guys seen Eliza?" he asked.

"She went back to your room to take a shower. Did you have fun in town?" his mother asked.

"Yes, it was eventful." He didn't linger. Turning on his heel, he made his way upstairs. Ever since Trudy had brought home Caroline, his family seemed to tread on eggshells around him.

He had no feelings for Caroline, not now, not ever. His sister had still yet to come out. Seeing as she'd interrupted his and Eliza's moment, sneaking her own girlfriend into the sun house, he had a feeling she had no intention of telling them.

Preston walked into the bedroom.

The bathroom door was still open, and he flicked the lock on the door. After kicking off his shoes, he sat down on the edge of the bed and waited.

He glanced at the time, hearing the shower turn

off. Eliza hummed to herself. He waited, tense, and with every passing second, he ran Melinda's words through his head repeatedly.

Eliza finally entered the bedroom and came to a stop with a jolt and a gasp. "Preston, I didn't know you were back home. I wouldn't have taken so long in the shower."

"I want to fuck you," he said.

Eliza froze, her hand holding her towel as if it was a lifeline. "Mr. Boone, this is deeply inappropriate."

"I cannot get you out of my head. Don't use my title. We both know you haven't been treating me as your boss. I'm not taking advantage of you. I'm not going to give you an ultimatum. Your job is secure and safe. You know this."

"This is ... that's a line we cannot cross."

"Why not?" he asked.

"You know why not." She sighed. "Sex complicates everything. I like working for you, Preston."

"Your job isn't going to be in question, Eliza."

"What about when the sex finishes?" she asked. "What then? When I have to go back to getting you jewelry for someone else. Do you think that's going to be easy for me?"

"Why do you feel this has to end?"

"Everything has to end at some point," she said.

He stood up and moved toward her. Eliza held herself straight.

"I felt how much you wanted me," he said. He stroked a curl of wet hair back from her face. "I liked the way you felt against me. I've been thinking of nothing else, and every time I do, I get hard just imagining it." He leaned close so his lips were right next to her ear. "I think about tasting your pussy, Eliza. I know you're going to taste good, and I know you're going to be the perfect fit on my rock-hard cock."

"Stop," she said, moaning and leaning a little into him. "We shouldn't do this."

"Tell me you haven't thought about me. Tell me that you don't think about what it would be like to be with me. Have you wondered how I'd feel inside you? Kissing you. Fucking you. Tasting you." He pressed her up against the wall, putting his hands at either side of her head, but touching her with only his body. He thrust his pelvis against her, letting her feel just how hard he was. "Do you feel that? I'm rock-hard for you. All I want is you. I don't think of anyone else but you."

He wanted to give in. To truly touch her, to finally taste her, but instead, he pulled back.

Eliza gasped.

"I'm not going to force you, Eliza. I'm telling you what I want. It's your turn to take the next step." With that, he turned on his heel and left the bedroom.

The ball was in Eliza's court. There was only so much he was willing to do.

Chapter Thirteen

Eliza had been good.

All her life.

The perfect daughter. The model student. The most efficient and hard-working employee she could be. No one could ever doubt her ability to do the right thing, to be the right person. To follow all the rules.

Then Preston had to go and do that to her, and now she was all over the place. His touch had set her on fire. Since that day in the sun house, where she'd felt his hands on her body. She was more than willing to throw caution to the wind, but his sister found them. It had brought with it a hard dose of reality.

She'd avoided him, successfully, in the hope of being able to gain back her senses, but it hadn't happened. Nope, she was the one still struggling, like always.

Now he had told her he wanted to fuck her, and damn it, her willpower could only last so long.

Calling her friends was out of the question. They already had money on how long this would all take to fall apart, and she didn't want to give them the satisfaction of knowing the truth.

Preston didn't demand an answer that night, or even the next day. It was only during breakfast two days after his confrontation, that he announced they were going to check out a house with Lydia.

This was news to her. She had a piece of toast in her mouth as she looked at him.

"You're looking at a house?" Marsha asked.

"I was surprised myself. It's the one at the end of the street. You know, the one I've been struggling to sell," Lydia said.

He hadn't said anything to her about looking at a

house.

Marsha looked like she was going to burst into tears.

"What does this mean, son?" Greg asked.

"I don't know yet. I've got to check the place out. See if I even like it and then if it all goes well, I'll make a decision." He had a smile on his face. If he was to move back to Westcliffe Heights, what did this mean for her? For their agreement?

Don't think about this now.

"What about you, Eliza? You seem shocked," Roger said.

"I'm fine." She forced a smile to her lips.

"I think it's good news," Caroline said. "I know Trudy has missed having her big brother around."

Each time Caroline spoke at the table, the entire family tensed, apart from Trudy and Preston. They were the ones who knew the truth, and so did she.

Eliza turned toward Caroline. "Would you like to join us?"

"No, she can't," Trudy said. "I'm taking Caroline out for the day."

The tension slowly eased.

Eliza finished her toast but didn't eat anything else.

When they left the table, she followed Preston to the front door to find Lydia waiting for them. "Do you guys want to walk or drive?" Lydia asked.

Preston took Eliza's hand, locking their fingers together. Again, she felt the heat and warmth from his touch. She didn't pull away.

"We can walk."

"Excellent. While we walk, I will tell you more about the property." Lydia filled the silence, but Eliza ignored her.

She'd stopped calling her friends. She hadn't spoken to them in over a week for fear they would know something was wrong. They had her back through everything. They would try to come down here to offer her support, and right now, she needed to stay focused in the role she'd agreed.

The only problem was she hated pretending.

Preston was a great guy. Each minute she spent in Westcliffe, seeing him with his family, she knew the truth. The businessman was the fake. Preston Boone, Westcliffe Heights guy, he was the real deal.

They arrived at a large property with iron gates. Lydia inserted the key and flicked the lock.

"Now, if you do decide to take this property on, there is a code you can use and you don't have to keep getting out of your car to unlock the gates. We've currently disabled it so we can keep it locked." Lydia let them both inside, closing the gate behind her. "It doesn't automatically lock, but you can decide to do that."

The front gardens were so beautiful. There were flower beds on each side of the path. The lawn had been perfectly mowed. It looked like the kind of house that would be on the front of a magazine.

They walked up several steps, moving around the corner and coming toward the opening of the house.

Three more steps brought them to the front door. The house had brick posts on either side, and Lydia opened the front door.

"Honestly, this place is incredible, and I'm not just saying that. It's shocking that no one has taken this," Lydia said.

Stepping into the front door, Eliza fell in love. It was straight out of her fantasies of a dream house. "Oh, my," Eliza said.

"Tell me about it," Lydia said.

It was a huge, open hallway, and she could see a large Christmas tree during the festive season, or some large spider for Halloween, along with cobwebs. The stairs were a few feet away, but as she turned left or right, she could see into the rooms.

Lydia took the lead, showing them a large, open dining room that led into the kitchen. They went through the sitting rooms, into an office, and there was a laundry room and a small pantry as well. The yard was big and long. There was a small yard past the main one with a couple of trees, and she could imagine her own kids with treehouses of their own.

There was a great deal of privacy, and there was also a small pool, which she loved.

"Let's head upstairs," Lydia said. "Now, compared to the other houses on this street, this one has only four bedrooms and two bathrooms. One of them is the en-suite to the master bedroom."

Eliza fell in love with the house. She never wanted a home to be so large that a family could seem to be living on their own. This place was everything she had ever wanted.

"I can see that you like it," Lydia said.

"It's amazing."

"Then I'll take it," Preston said. "If Eliza likes it, tell me what I need to sign."

She froze. This wasn't hers and Preston's dream house. They were not actually engaged. The ring she wore was a fake. The bracelet she'd been wearing was a mockery of the potential for vows.

Eliza tugged on his hand. "Don't you think you need to look at this place a little more? Get a good look at everything. Not just ... make a rash decision."

Lydia's cell phone went off. "Shoot, I need to take this." She stepped out of the bedroom.

Eliza watched her go.

"What's the problem, Eliza?"

"Don't you think you're making a rash decision?" she asked. "They're going to think you're making the decision for me."

"What if I am?" he asked.

"Don't do that. Don't pretend like this is something more than it actually is. We both know—"

"I've got to go. If I give you the keys, I'll get the paperwork together and we can handle it back at your parents?" Lydia asked.

"Sure thing."

Lydia pressed the keys into his hands, gave him a smile, and left them alone.

Eliza heard the door close and she nibbled on her lip as she glanced around the large master bedroom. "You want this house?" Eliza asked.

"Why is it so hard for you to believe?"

"I've been inside your bachelor pad back at the city. Believe me, this place is a far cry from anything you have back there."

"And it seems so far out of my reach?"

She frowned. "No, of course not."

"Then what's the problem?"

"I don't know. This place just doesn't seem you."

He snorted. "So you're judging me based on what you think you know of me."

"No, I'm judging you based on what I know."

"Really? So you knew about my parents. The love that has lasted since they were ten years old. You knew I had three brothers, all married. A sister who is gay, and still hasn't come out to my parents."

"No, I didn't know all of that."

"Okay, then how about this. Did you know all my life I've wanted a big family? How I cannot wait to be the dad that has screaming kids around the table and he can't think straight? Or the fact I want to hold a baby in my arms? That I love to snuggle? How I want to get a couple of dogs and have the time to train them?" he asked.

Her mouth opened. "You want that?"

"Yes, I do."

She looked around the room before directing her gaze straight at him. "How? Why?"

"Why did I leave town and go and build my company?"

"Wasn't there someone here you wanted to love?" she asked.

"No. I never had a girlfriend here. I lost my virginity at a party in college."

"How old?" she asked.

"Twenty-one years old."

This did surprise her. "You're quite the enigma, Preston," she said.

He took a step toward her. "Eliza, I'm pretty sure there are a lot of things you don't know about me. Don't believe everything you see or read. You got questions, come ask me."

"Why me?" she asked.

She had no intention of asking him that, but the words just slipped out before she could stop them, and the moment they were out, she cringed. This wasn't a topic she wanted to talk about.

He reached out and slowly stroked back some hair. "Why not you? You know I told my family that it was your ass I saw?" he asked.

She felt her cheeks beginning to heat. "I might remember that."

He leaned in close so his lips brushed against her cheek. "I'm going to tell you something else."

Eliza held her breath, waiting.

"I wasn't lying."

He pulled back, and she couldn't stop looking at his lips.

"This is wrong," she said.

"Does it feel wrong?" he asked.

"No."

"We're two consenting adults. I'm not using my power over you or blackmailing you. I'm telling you, Eliza, that I'm attracted to you."

She couldn't be held responsible for what she did.

Throwing her arms around his waist, she slammed her lips down on his. It was awkward and somewhat jerky, but Preston caught her, holding her tight within his arms. The firmness of his hands held her steady, and she gasped when they moved down to touch her ass. The way he squeezed her, it sent an answering pulse straight between her legs.

"We can't do this here," she said.

"Lydia isn't coming back. I'm going to buy this place, and I don't want to wait another minute."

She didn't hesitate. Grabbing his shirt, she tore it from his body as he grabbed hers. Within seconds, they were naked and she was on the bed.

"Do you have any idea how fucking gorgeous you are?" His lips grazed across each of her tits before he took one of her nipples into his mouth. This couldn't be happening. Her boss was sucking on her breasts.

This kind of thing happened in the movies, not in real life, and yet, here she was, aroused, panting for more, hungry for him, desperate, and not wanting him to stop.

He kissed between the valley of her breasts, going down toward her pussy. No man had ever kissed her between the legs before.

"You don't have to do that," she said.

Preston looked up at her. "I want to."

Oh, boy.

****

His cock was hard as fucking rock.

Eliza's body was so full, so ripe, so ready to take him. Preston ran his hands over her body, feeling the fullness of her hips, the thickness of her thighs, and he basked in every single inch of her.

She was a prize. He couldn't believe he'd waited this long to have a taste. Kissing down her stomach, he got closer to her pussy.

He'd never liked women who shaved between the legs. He wanted to be with a woman, not a girl. Cupping her mound, he slid his fingers between her slit and found her soaking wet.

She cried out.

Preston didn't know why she didn't want this. He couldn't get enough. Staring down at her, all he wanted to do was drive his cock in deep and fill her with his cum.

Instead, he kissed the inside of her thigh.

She sighed.

He went to the other leg and did the same. Holding the lips of her sex, he spread her open and licked across her clit. She nearly came up off the bed.

"Wow," she said. "I ... er ... I've never done that before."

"Done what? You're not a virgin, are you?"

She shook her head. "I'm not a virgin but ... I ... no man has ever ... you know." Her face was bright red.

"No man has tasted you?"

"No."

He smiled. "Then lie back because you're in for a hell of a fun time." He licked his lips, more than prepared to let her know what she'd been missing.

Eliza lay back down, and he went back to licking at her clit. He started light, using just the tip of his tongue to graze across her clit. Each touch had her jerking. He kept his fingers on her pussy.

Preston teased down toward her entrance, skimming over her pussy. She tasted so good. He couldn't get enough of her.

When she stopped jerking with each stroke, he used the flat of his tongue, driving up and down her clit.

Her moans became louder, and she started to thrust her pussy onto his face. He moved his hands from the lips of her sex, sliding underneath to grab the curves of her ass. Then he pressed his face against her pussy, lapping her up.

"I'm close," Eliza said. Her pants filled the air.

He sucked her clit into his mouth, and as she came, his name spilled from her mouth, echoing through the room.

Preston kept on going with his light touches, prolonging her orgasm. When she could no longer stand his touch, he kissed her clit and leaned back. He reached into his jeans, going for his wallet where he stashed a condom.

After tearing into the foil, he removed the rubber and slowly worked it over his length. He was so hard.

Eliza had moved up onto her elbows.

"There will be time to linger. To touch. To do a hell of a lot more later, but I can't wait. I've got to feel you now," he said.

Eliza moved back as he crawled up the bed, following her until he lay between her spread thighs. He put his cock to her entrance, and slowly, inch by inch, he began to slide inside her.

She was tight and so wet.

He wanted there to be nothing between them. To feel her warmth surrounding him. She wrapped her arms around his waist, her hands dropping to the curve of his waist as well as her legs.

Pressing one hand beside her head, with the other, he gripped her thigh and slammed the last few inches to the hilt. They both cried out.

He felt her pussy tighten around him. Each little flutter making his own arousal bigger.

"Fuck," he said.

"What is it?" she asked.

"You have no idea how amazing you feel."

He slammed his lips down on hers and rocked slowly within her. It had been a long time for him. He'd been taking care of his arousal with his hand, and he didn't know how much longer he could stand. He wasn't some teenage boy, and yet, inside Eliza's body, he didn't feel like a grown-ass man.

Gritting his teeth, he tried to keep control, but with every thrust, he felt his own orgasm building.

There was no stopping it. He handled a total of four thrusts, and much to his shame, he slammed inside her and pulsed deep inside her pussy. Even before he finished, embarrassment flooded him. Breaking the kiss, he stared into her eyes, shocked. Not even on his first time had he come so quickly.

Eliza nibbled on her lip.

"It's not supposed to be like that."

"It's fine," she said. "Honestly, we better leave this house before someone comes and views it."

"No." His cock had gone slightly flaccid, but he was more than ready to go again. "I don't have any more condoms with me."

"Preston, it's fine."

"No, it's not fine. I'm better than this."

She smiled. "I ... er ... I came again. I'm not mocking you. It's just that it has been a whole long time, and well, I guess I wasn't expecting this, and with your tongue and everything, I mean, wow."

He frowned down at her, then he felt it. The tiny ripples of her release. "Oh."

This had to be the most awkward of experiences in his life.

"I enjoyed it," she said.

"Good."

She pressed her lips together. "Do you think we can ... you know, get out of here?"

"Do you like the house?" he asked.

"I love it. You don't need my approval to buy this."

He was about to tell her he wanted her approval regardless, but then her cell phone started to ring.

Preston had no choice but to pull out of her as she scrambled toward the side of the bed.

"It's work," she said.

He watched as she reached into her jeans and pulled out the work cell phone.

"Hello, Mr. Aguire," she said.

He tensed up.

Work had been the last thing on his mind since he entered this home. He did the necessary emails and stuff that required his urgent attention, but for the most part, he'd been so heavily focused on enjoying Eliza's company and being back home.

"The end of this week? Sure, we can do that. Where would you like to meet?" Eliza asked.

She turned to him and gave him the name of a hotel that was just on the outskirts of town.

He nodded his head, and she finished making the necessary arrangements.

She finished the call and sat at the edge of the bed.

"Don't do it," he said. "Don't think too hard."

He kissed her neck.

"All I can do is think right now." She bent down and began to gather her clothes, getting dressed. "I'm not being … I don't know what I'm being right now, but I've got to head back to the house."

"Eliza?"

"I've got to get whatever I need faxed or emailed over," Eliza said. "I totally forgot to bring the file, but don't worry about it. I've got this."

"Eliza."

"Preston, please, I need some space. That's all."

He sighed.

Getting dressed, he didn't like this new distance she'd created.

They left the property, and he made sure to lock the gate behind them.

"I'm going to head into town," he said.

"Okay, I'll see you back at the house later."

She turned away from him, and he gritted his teeth, hands clenched at his sides. Eliza was an enigma.

Spinning on his heel, he started his way toward town, going straight toward the pharmacy. That one time with Eliza was never going to be enough, so he went and got some reinforcements, condoms.

He wanted to fuck her again. To get under her skin the way she had him. What he wanted more than anything was for her to loosen up.

Just as he was leaving the pharmacy, he saw a salon named Juliet's, and instantly, his thoughts went to her best friends. He pulled out his cell phone. Unbeknownst to Eliza, her friends were not kidding when it came to taking care of their girl. They'd saved their numbers into his cell phone.

Scrolling through his contact list, he saw Juliet's name and dialed it. After five rings, it went to voicemail, promising to get back in touch. He hung up, not wanting to leave a message, and went straight for Mackenzie's number.

She answered on the second ring.

"Hello?" she asked.

"Mackenzie, it's Preston."

"Who?"

"Eliza's boss."

"Ah, right the one working her to the bone right now so she can't call us?"

"What?" he asked. "Eliza hasn't called you?"

"Not once in the past week. Do you want to tell us what's going on there?"

"Nothing's going on." He groaned.

"Something is going on and Eliza is avoiding because she doesn't want us to get involved. Do you want Juliet and me to come down there?" Mackenzie asked.

"No, I don't think that's entirely necessary just yet."

"Okay, so if you didn't know about Eliza not talking to us, and you weren't calling to warn us about something, why are you calling me?"

He pressed his lips together. "I need your help."

"With what?"

"I ... I want Eliza to fall for me."

There was silence on the line.

Preston glanced down at his cell phone before putting it back to his ear. "Are you still there?"

"Yeah, yeah, I'm here. I just, I guess I wasn't expecting that for an answer."

"Yeah, I guess so."

"Has something happened between you and Eliza?" Mackenzie asked.

Preston smiled at a couple of the neighbors. "What does that have to do with anything?"

"Holy crap, something happened. Didn't it? I just knew it."

"I don't know if anything happened."

"Did you two sleep together?" Mackenzie said.

He was starting to wish he hadn't called Mackenzie at all. "You know what, how about I just hang up and we both forget about this conversation."

"Wait? What? Hell no. If you've got feelings for Eliza, then I need to know what they are. Juliet and I need to know if we have to come and kick your ass."

"Do you know if Eliza is attracted to me?" he asked. He wanted to slap his head against the nearest post to wake some sense into him. He was a grown man and he was asking his woman's best friends if she even liked him.

She's not your woman yet.

Mackenzie smiled. "Well, that depends if you've got the ten."

"The ten?"

Mackenzie sighed. "It is a list of ten things Eliza cooked up that were important factors toward her falling for her man."

"Ten?"

Woman of ten.

"Yeah."

"What are they?"

"Oh, please, I'm not telling you all of her ten. Besides the fact I don't know. We all did it. It was something we did after we all got our hearts broken and it sucked big time. Anyway, I'm not going to tell you. Just know that you are more suited to Eliza than you would believe. Next time you see her, tell her to pick up her phone, and also, yes, Eliza is attracted to you. She's had a crush on you for years, but she would never say anything."

He was still reeling from the *ten* comment.

Eliza had made a list of ten things.

No, there was no way Eliza was the woman from Melinda's prediction.

Woman of ten.

No. Not happening.

There were limits to what he accepted about Melinda's premonition. Being back in town was weakening his resolve. It couldn't be possible. He refused to believe it.

Running a hand down his face, he made his way into the house only to find no one around. There was no sign of his parents or siblings.

What the hell was he going to do?

Chapter Fourteen

I've had sex with my boss.
I've had very good sex with my boss.
No, it was adequate.
Not life-changing.

I had sex with my boss.

Eliza cringed.

Her cell phone went off as she continued to pace in her and Preston's room. His parents had gone out, as had all of his siblings, leaving her alone in the house. After getting the necessary files faxed to her, and doing everything Eliza Drake would do, she'd come up to this bedroom to pack.

Then she'd freaked out.

Walking out on Preston now would be a huge mistake.

A massive one.

He didn't deserve that.

She'd stuffed her suitcase back in the closet and put her clothes back in order. Why couldn't her life be simple? Where she worked her ass off, then came back to her apartment, hung out with Juliet and Mackenzie, or made something. She liked to work with her hands. It helped her to think.

"I'm an idiot." She sat on the edge of the bed took a deep breath.

Her cell phone went off again and she saw it was Mackenzie calling her. The last five calls had been from her friend.

Guilt filled her as she thought about how she'd been the last week without her friends. They didn't deserve her silence either. She'd been an awful friend.

Accepting the call, she pressed it against her ear.

"Hi," she said.

"You had sex with your boss?"

Eliza gasped. "What? How did you know?"

There was some hesitation, a couple of stumbled words. "That doesn't matter how I know. I just know. It's why you haven't been calling, isn't it?"

"Preston called you."

"That's beside the point."

"No, it's not," Eliza said. "It is the whole point. The only way you could know that I had sex with my boss is if he called you. Did he?"

Mackenzie sighed. "Yes, we exchanged numbers with him because we were looking out for you."

"Does Juliet know?"

"I've sent her a text. Please, tell me why you sound miserable."

The door to the bedroom opened, and Preston stepped inside.

"I have to go right now. I will talk to you soon, okay."

"Wait, Eliza, he wanted to know how to get you to fall for him. I told him about the ten and that he should ask you."

"Huh, what?" Mackenzie hung up, and Eliza looked at Preston.

"I take it that was Mackenzie?" he asked.

"You called her."

Preston closed the door. "We're alone." He still flicked the lock into place.

That one action should not have her aroused, and yet, her nipples puckered. The sex they shared had been good. Not groundbreaking, but it was nice. She'd been just as into it, and it wasn't like she lasted a long time. She had checked, and they had each reached orgasm within fifteen minutes of starting.

Preston's tongue was a deadly weapon. There

was no way he should be allowed to go anywhere with that thing.

"Everyone had errands to run and stuff to do." She reached for the Aguire file. "I got the notes we're going to need."

"I don't care about work." He threw a box onto the bed, and she turned to see it was a multi-pack of condoms.

"You went shopping."

"I have never been more embarrassed than I was today." He started to open his shirt, button by button.

She licked her lips, seeing his chest as he removed his shirt.

He stepped up to her, and she didn't fight him as he started to remove her shirt. There was no rush in his. She dropped her cell phone to the floor as he pushed her shirt off her shoulders. He spun her toward him so her back was flush with his chest. Then he flicked the catch of her bra, dispensing with it in the same fashion as he had with her shirt.

When he got to her shorts, she expected him to remove them, but instead, his hand moved down to cup her between her thighs.

She leaned back, resting her head against his shoulder. The moan didn't stay trapped in her throat, but came out.

"Tell me you don't want me, and I'll stop all of this," he said.

She kept her lips closed.

"I don't want just one taste, Eliza." He reached up, flicking the button of her shorts. When she arrived back home after being with Preston the first time, she'd changed into the shorts as they felt more comfortable in the heat of summer.

It didn't matter what she was wearing. With

Preston removing her clothes, they were soon on the floor with her panties.

Sometime during the process, he'd removed his jeans and boxer briefs. He came up behind her, naked, the hard ridge of his cock pressing into her back.

His hands went to her hips, sliding around her stomach, then moving up. He moved his lips up to her neck, kissing right over her pulse. Her nipples tightened at the contact, a moan falling from her mouth as he cupped her tits.

Preston pinched her nipples at the same time his teeth sank against her neck. She cried out. The pleasure shot straight to her pussy, lighting her on fire.

"I can do so much better, Eliza."

He let go of her breasts, moving down her stomach and going between her thighs to stroke her clit. He didn't linger as he moved down toward her cunt, sliding in a single finger, followed by a second. "I want this pussy to belong to me."

She closed her eyes and nodded.

His thumb stroked over her clit. He pulled his hand from her pussy, and she opened her eyes, watching as he lifted his fingers to his mouth and licked each digit, tasting her, one by one.

She was shocked that he did this.

"I want to taste your pussy again," he said.

All she could do was jerk her head. She didn't know what had happened to Preston, but she had no problem with his commanding tone.

He placed her on the edge of the bed, told her to keep her thighs open, and then, he knelt between her legs. "I want you to watch," he said.

Preston put her hands on her knees. "Keep them there."

She looked down as he moved between her

thighs, his tongue touching her pussy. He pressed two fingers deep inside her, and she moaned. Her hands clenched tight around her knees as he started to lick at her pussy.

This wasn't fair.

She hadn't been ready.

But under his touch, she forgot about him being her boss. Her worries ebbed away, and she focused on the moment, on being with Preston. The man who was a true mystery to her. The same man he kept hidden from the rest of the world. She didn't mind the asshole he was, so long as it wasn't directed at her. There was nothing she hated more than to be reprimanded by him, but seeing him unleash the asshole in the boardroom, well, that was a thing of beauty.

Eliza arched up, moaning as his tongue swept over her pussy. He was making her addicted to oral. She'd never been with a man who wanted to go down on her, but the way he sucked at her pussy and his hands gripped her ass as if he couldn't get enough of her, she knew she'd been missing out.

"You taste so good."

She cried out as he took her clit into his mouth and used his teeth around her nub. He bit down just hard enough that it was almost too much, but as he pressed his tongue to her clit, she relaxed against him, whimpering.

Preston did this a couple more times before, flicking his tongue back and forth across her clit. Each stroke built her orgasm, and when she thought she was just about to topple over the edge, he withdrew, sliding his tongue toward her entrance as he began to use it to fuck her. Shallow strokes.

She shook with need. Hungry with it.

"You taste so good," he said. He took his time, tasting her.

She was so wet, she felt herself dripping from her pussy between her ass cheeks.

Finally, he moved back to her clit, and this time, as her orgasm began to build, he didn't stop, not once.

He threw her over the edge into one of the best orgasms she'd ever had. Eliza didn't even think it was possible to feel this good. Her body felt amazing. She didn't want it to stop. This was life-changing. She moaned his name, sinking her fingers into his hair as she thrust her pelvis against his face.

Preston didn't stop. He kept on licking her pussy, and before she knew what was happening, he'd sent her into a second orgasm. This one wasn't as hard and as deep as the first, but it was enough to have her gasping for more. He kissed between her legs and moved up between them.

She watched as he took a condom and tore into the foil. The simple action of his teeth against the wrapping shouldn't have turned her on, but it did. She even liked the way he slid the latex over his cock.

He was so hard, the vein seeming to throb against the side of his cock. Within seconds, he had the condom on. Eliza moved up the bed, but Preston captured her ankle and pulled her back down until she was a little further onto the bed than the edge.

The hard tip of his cock slid between her slit. Each time he bumped her clit, she cried out, arching up, offering her tits to Preston, and he took complete advantage.

With one hand on the bed, keeping him upright, he used his other to stroke across the curve of her breast. He pinched her nipple before he took one into his mouth.

She'd never found her breasts so erotic, but as he tugged on her nipple, an answering call happened between her legs that made her moan for more.

He let go of her tit, reached down between them, and inch by inch, he pressed inside her. Preston wasn't small by any means, and as he took his time thrusting inside her, Eliza got to feel every single inch.

He wasn't all the way inside her, but he grabbed her hands and pressed them on either side of the bed, keeping her locked in place.

His gaze was on hers. Elia couldn't look away even if she wanted to, and there was no way she did.

With the last couple of inches, he held himself poised, in no rush to get it over with.

She watched him, mesmerized.

She licked her lips, and that action must have triggered something within him because he tightened his whole body and slammed balls deep inside her, hitting a part of herself she'd never been touched before. It was almost too painful and pleasurable at the same time.

Preston held himself there for several seconds before he started to pull back. He didn't give her enough time to recover before he was doing it all over again.

He took his time, making her get used to the feel of his cock, and there was no denying he was glorious.

When she began to thrust up to meet him, he started to really fuck her. With each thrust, she felt another orgasm start to begin, but it was like Preston was proving to her that today was a fluke.

He pulled out of her, flipped her over with ease so that she was on her knees, and was once against inside her.

If she thought he was deep before, then she was wrong. At this angle, he went to a part of her she didn't even know she had. It was highly pleasurable, and with it, she couldn't contain herself.

His name spilled from her lips, echoing around the room.

Preston ran his hands up her body, cupping her tits, using them at odd times as leverage as he took what he wanted.

She gave her body to him, needing to come, and as his hand dived between her legs, she didn't think it was possible, but this was Preston Boone. This man didn't take no for an answer, and he proved it as he fingered her into another orgasm, only with this one, he followed her with his own.

Eliza felt each time his cock twitched as he came.

Not only had she now had sex with her boss once, this was twice, and she wanted to do it again, so many times.

****

"Don't you think we should talk about what we're going to do with Aguire?" Eliza said.

Preston smirked as he traced the path down her back. "Nope."

She turned her head. "You're just going to wing it?"

"I don't even know what the man wants to discuss."

Eliza reached behind her and grabbed a pillow, pulling it against her body as she turned to look at him.

He didn't like her hiding her body from him. After coming home and taking her once, they had both had a shower, where he'd taken her a second time, then a third. His cock was already raring to go for a fourth.

Eliza seemed determined to want to discuss business, which he was in no mood for.

"Preston, you guys want to talk about you buying his land. Can't you focus?" she asked.

"Eliza, I've got a very sexy, very naked woman in my bed. I don't care about acquiring any land other than this." He snatched the pillow from the front of her body and placed his hand between her thighs, feeling how wet she was for him.

"You've already proven you're amazing in bed."

"I'm not here to prove anything. I want you, Eliza." He kissed her lips, then trailed down to her neck. "Don't you want me?"

She grabbed his shoulders, and this time, she surprised him as she pushed him to the bed.

Preston had no problem with the sudden change of events as she straddled his waist. Her hands went to his chest, pushing him down.

He put his hands on her knees, stroking up, then reaching for her hips. Preston couldn't get enough of her body. He loved how full she was. She'd been able to handle every fuck, every thrust, all of him.

Cupping her tits, he traced his thumb over each peak, and she arched back. He gave them a little twist and lifted to take each one between his lips, to lick at them. To soothe out the pain he'd caused.

"We're never going to get any work done at this rate," she said.

"Good. I want you focused on me." Moving his hands to her back, he traced down, going straight to her ass.

She whimpered.

He didn't want to use a condom, but to feel her tight cunt wrapped around his cock. Would it be so hard not to have condoms?

Eliza pushed on his shoulders, and he got his answer as she reached for the box of condoms.

He lay back, spreading his arms wide. "You've got me, Eliza. You can do whatever the hell you want with me."

She snorted.

The condom was out of the packet, and she

tucked her long blonde locks behind her ear. She looked nervous.

"Pinch the tip," he said. "Then roll it over my cock."

She followed his instructions, then moved to straddle his waist. This time, he couldn't not touch her. Her body was perfection, and he grabbed her hips.

"You're going to have to put me inside you," he said.

Eliza lifted up, held the base of his cock, and he couldn't look away. Preston watched and felt at the same time as she slowly, inch by inch, sank on his length.

After he was balls deep inside her, she put her hands on his chest and closed her eyes. He didn't like that.

"Open your eyes. I want you to look at me. To know who's inside you."

She smiled. "Do you think I can forget?"

He thrust his pelvis up, and she gasped. "Fuck, that feels good," she said.

He grabbed her hips. "There's always more where that came from."

She chuckled. "I get it. You're hot in bed, but we've got to talk about work."

"No, we really don't."

"Preston."

"Eliza."

"Work has to come first."

"Fine, I have no interest in planning for our meeting with Aguire. I've gone that route, and to be honest, I no longer care if he allows me to buy his land. This will be on him. I'm going to have you with me, and that's all I'm going to do." He stroked her hips.

"I don't like the idea of lying to him."

"I don't either, which again, I'm not going to do

anything to make him think too much, okay? Now, can we get back to the business at hand?" he asked. "Fuck me or let me take over. I need to be inside you."

He went to sit up, but Eliza pushed him right back down.

"I didn't put you in charge. You've been in charge for way too long. It's time for us mere mortals to have a turn."

With her hands on his chest, she took her sweet time, but he had no problem with the way she rode his cock. Each stroke seemed to take him a little deeper, but what he loved most was seeing her come apart. The way her eyes closed, but then she'd flutter them open, almost as if it was an afterthought.

He couldn't stop touching her.

He didn't want to.

Eliza rocked on his cock, and even though he'd come for most of the day, seeing her like this, letting go, almost being naughty, fucking her boss, it was too much.

Preston let go of her hip and sucked on his thumb, getting it wet. After pressing his thumb between her thighs, he stroked over her clit, and she cried out, arching up, thrusting her tits out, and he felt her release.

He was a little surprised how quickly she came apart, but he loved watching her. Couldn't get enough of how she let go. There was nothing false in her reaction. She was all woman, every step of the way, and he was addicted.

Gripping her hips, he sped up her thrusts, and it didn't take long for him to join her in bliss. This time, he closed his eyes, feeling his cock and the way she milked him. It was such a shame they were using a condom.

Once they were finished, Eliza collapsed against him with a few little pants. "Wow," she said.

He chuckled. "Wow, right back at ya."

"I'm never like this," she said.

"Like what?"

"Sleeping with the boss. This is something I never, ever do."

He pressed a kiss to her shoulder. "After you've been working with me for three years, believe me, I already know. Let me take care of this condom."

Eliza moved off his cock, and he rolled off the bed, going into the bathroom. He was about to remove it when he saw his cum leaking out of the tip.

He grabbed some tissue, and as he placed the used condom on the tissue, he saw the tear in the tip of the condom.

Fuck.

Preston glanced back toward the door.

He had to tell her.

After rolling the condom up in the tissue, he tossed it into the trash, and then he grabbed the trash bin lining, sealing it up to lift it out.

You've got to tell her.

Heading back into the bedroom, he saw Eliza was laid on her front, her hair giving her the just-fucked appearance, and it was his fault. He couldn't get enough of running his fingers through the long length.

"What's up?"

"Er…"

Eliza had no idea.

She didn't even look suspicious. A soft smile played on her lips, and if he was to tell her the condom had broken, she'd lose all of that. She'd start to panic, look freaked out. She'd think about the premonition Melinda had given her, and with a busted condom, there was a chance.

The businessman within him, the sensible guy, was berating him to tell the truth. The guy who enjoyed

Eliza's company, who didn't want this to end and knew the busted condom would bring it to a swift end, didn't want to.

His selfish one over.

He placed the trash bin near the door and quickly pulled on a pair of sweats. "I'm starving. Are you hungry?"

"I could eat."

"I'll grab us some food."

"How about pizza?" Eliza asked.

"Pizza it will be, but I've got to wait for it to be delivered."

She smiled. "A sandwich will be more than fine."

He winked at her, then left the bedroom.

Guilt flooded him. This was the wrong thing to do. He knew that without a doubt.

Running a hand down his face, he went to the kitchen and out the back, finding the trash cans against the wall. He threw the bag into the trash one.

With the evidence now out of sight, he took a step back.

He pulled out his cell phone and dialed the local pizza place, putting in orders for a couple of pizzas.

Entering the house, he came to a stop when he saw his father at the kitchen counter, making a sandwich.

He and Eliza hadn't left the bedroom.

"Hey, Dad," he said.

"Hey, son. You missed dinner."

"Er, I know. I'm sorry."

"Don't worry about it. To be young and to be in love." Greg put a slice of cheese in the sandwich and took a bite.

Was that a clue to the fact his father didn't believe the lies?

"You know all about it," he said.

"I met an interesting man in town today. He's not from around here. Goes by the name Aguire. Know him?"

"Dad, you know I do."

"Yeah, he's quite excited to meet the newly engaged couple. You see, it was a little shock to me to learn of just how new this engagement was, and I then did the math. Tell me, son, what game are you playing?"

"I'm not playing any game."

"No? Because I don't like being lied to, and there are times Eliza has looked like a deer caught in headlights. Trust me, I know what that look is all about."

"You heard what Melinda said," Preston said.

"I also know that your company means everything to you. Even more than telling the truth to your own family."

"Eliza is my fiancée," he said. "Is it so hard for you to believe?"

"It wasn't until today."

Preston pressed his lips together and placed his hands on his hips. He didn't want his father to know the truth. He didn't want any of his family to know the truth. They adored Eliza and the truth was he needed to know what Mackenzie talked about when she said about her list of ten. He'd never considered himself a superstitious person, but between Eliza entering his life, the condom breaking, and Melinda messing with his head like that, it was hard not to see everything a little more clearly.

"Tell the truth, son."

"The truth?" he asked. Preston laughed. "The truth is this. Eliza entered my life as an employee. I pulled her out of a crowd, and from day one, she has done nothing but blow me away. She is amazing, crazy smart, funny, quirky, and above all else, she is loyal. Any man would be crazy to let her go." He licked his lips and stared at his father. "I love her. I don't want her to go away, ever." The doorbell rang. "That is the truth. Now if you'll excuse me, I've got to get some pizza."

He turned on his heel and went toward the door.

"Preston," Marsha said, coming downstairs.

"It's okay, Mom. I ordered pizza for me and Eliza."

He opened the door, and two middle-aged people stood on the doorstep.

"You're not pizza," he said.

Marsha burst out laughing, moving past him.

"Of course, it's not pizza, but your father and I, we didn't want you two love birds to wait, and I knew Eliza would love to see her parents."

"Mom? Dad?"

Preston turned to see Eliza walking downstairs, a robe covering her naked body.

Her hair was pulled across one shoulder, and she looked so sexy. He wanted her again.

The words he said to his father came back to haunt him as he looked at her. The cold, harsh truth finally dawning on him when he realized that he hadn't lied to his father. He had fallen in love with Eliza. It hadn't happened overnight but had been a gradual process. One he hadn't seen coming. He didn't know exactly when it started, but he knew long ago he didn't like her going on dates. It was one of the many reasons he'd sabotage any chance of her having a life outside of work.

With each step she took, she looked a little paler.

"Hey, sweetheart. We had to come and be part of your wedding. Mr. and Mrs. Boone came and told us their plans of organizing you both an amazing wedding that would also correlate with their own anniversary."

Eliza was pulled away from him and into a hug.

Oh, shit.

Chapter Fifteen

Eliza sat on the edge of the bed, feeling the panic rise.

"Just breathe. It's going to be okay." Preston rubbed at her back, and she shook her head.

This was getting to be oh, so real.

With a hand on her chest, she tried to control her breathing. She leaned forward, putting her head between her legs, and started to try to count to ten, or to do anything else that would not panic her.

"My parents are here," she said.

"I know."

"They're going to organize a real wedding."

"I got that."

She lifted up and glared at him. "Please stop answering my points. I'm not saying them as a question."

"I figured if I talked to you, you'd stop freaking out and we could approach this calmly," he said.

Down her head went.

"There is no calm. There is only panic. Oh, my God, my mom is here. My dad too. They saw me coming downstairs pretty much naked."

"You were not naked."

"I totally was and you know it. I didn't have any clothes on beneath the robe and they would have seen. Oh, God, they know."

Preston didn't run away. His palm was on her back, rubbing up and down.

Marsha had come to the room while they were waiting for pizza and asked her if she had a moment because she wanted to talk.

She hadn't questioned it. There was no way she was going to be rude to Preston's parents.

Seeing her mom and dad, she felt sick again.

"Oh, God, they are going to know. This is a disaster."

"They're not going to know, Eliza. Trust me. We've got this. We're not going to be told when we're getting married. Don't worry."

She lifted up and then started to laugh. "You don't get parents, do you?"

"What is there to get? This is our life."

"You're telling me you're happy to completely disappoint them?" she asked. "To go down there and tell them that we're not getting married. That you and I already have a plan?"

"Yes."

"You're on your own."

There was a knock at their door.

Eliza ran her fingers through her hair. The moment she had excused herself, she'd pulled on a pair of sweatpants and one of Preston's large shirts. She wasn't going to acknowledge how nice it smelled.

The only two people she truly took advice from were back in the city. Hours from where she was. They would help her see sense, but if they knew her parents were already here, they'd come down. They wouldn't help her, but they would help prepare the parties.

"This is a nightmare."

She got herself together, remembering Preston still needed her to play a part, and forced a smile to her lips as he opened the door.

Trudy held two pizza boxes.

"These are for you. I'm to tell you that they are deep in organizing the wedding. I think they've already sent out the invitations."

"Now would be a good time to talk about Caroline," Preston said.

"No way. I'm not spoiling this big day for you."

"Caroline, you owe me."

"Look, they're excited to be organizing your wedding. Do you know how worried Mom and Dad have been about you?"

"I imagine it's the same for the both of us. It always shocks me how you can get away with everything and I cannot."

"Preston, don't start."

Eliza got to her feet. "Please, do not argue."

Trudy sighed. "You two deserve your happiness."

"And you don't with Caroline?" Preston asked.

"I will tell them when it's the right time."

Preston snorted.

Eliza shook her head. "I don't think I can handle this." She took the pizzas from Trudy and placed them on the floor.

Sitting down, she opened one up and didn't care there was pineapple on top. Juliet was the lover of pineapple on a pizza. After tearing off the slice, she cupped her hand and took a large bite.

She closed her eyes, enjoying all the flavors. "This is a good pizza."

"Westcliffe Heights has the best of everything," Trudy said.

"Totally." She took another bite of pizza. There was nothing in this world that couldn't be solved by pizza or pasta. That was her motto, or at least it was going to be.

Lifting her head, she looked at Trudy.

"Tell me, are they talking wedding dresses?" Eliza asked.

Trudy sighed and bit her lip.

"Just tell me."

"Your mom brought her wedding dress. Apparently, it's part of your wedding."

Eliza groaned.

"And there is a list your mother wants you to remember," Trudy said.

"List?" she and Preston asked together.

"Yeah, she said that it was something you, Mackenzie, and Juliet did as you were kids. She started to ask Mom a whole load of questions about Preston, but then decided she didn't know all of the details and so she, er, called reinforcements."

She looked toward Preston to find his stare a little strange. It was like he was trying to figure something out.

"Reinforcements?"

"Your friends are coming here."

Eliza dropped the pizza and crawled across the floor, going to her cell phone. Unlocking the screen, she went to her apartment's number.

No answer.

Juliet.

No answer.

Mackenzie.

No answer.

"She's right. They're coming here." Eliza groaned. "We need alcohol."

"Are you two really engaged?" Trudy asked.

"Yes," Preston said, glaring at his sister. "We had our own plan for when we were going to get married. A Christmas wedding was what we talked about." He took a seat, tearing off a slice of pizza.

"It was going to be beautiful," Eliza said. She wanted to cry.

"Look, you know how our parents can be," Trudy said. "They always think they know best. If it makes you feel any better, Roger, Andrew, and Kian didn't get any of the plans they wanted either." Trudy sighed. "I'm going to leave you two alone to enjoy your pizza fest."

She made her escape pretty quickly.

Eliza crawled back toward the pizza, resting her back against the bed. "We're doomed, aren't we?"

"Not yet. I will not call us defeated yet."

"You're going to hold out a little longer?" Eliza asked.

"I was wondering if you could tell me about this list." He'd already finished one slice and had moved into a second.

She sighed. "It was … stupid."

"Do you know what was on that list?"

"Of course. It was … we'd had a bad experience with some guys, okay? I decided to make a list so I would never defer from that list." She blew out a breath. "If I tell you this, you cannot, under any circumstance, repeat it, mock me, or use it against me."

He held his hands up. "I won't do any of those things."

"Okay, well, the first one is kind of silly, but I like it. It's quirky and that is he has to love different flavored pancakes. They have to be weird as well."

"Like banana?" he asked.

"Exactly." She chuckled. She was not trying to draw attention to the fact he held some of the attributes to her ten items. "The next one is pretty easy. He's got to be a family man who wants dozens of kids. That could be any guy, right? Most people want kids." She tore off another pizza slice. "Loves to snuggle is another, and that goes into the next point of being good in bed. I think every woman should want that from her guy. No one wants a boring man in bed."

He raised a brow.

"I'm moving way off topic." She wasn't about to tell him that so far, he had every single point. He was a family man, and he'd admitted to her wanting kids.

"Intelligent."

"You want an intelligent man?" he asked.

"Yes. A guy who is good in bed and who makes me want to talk out of it. That's not so hard to imagine, is it?" She glared at him. When she'd been making the list, Juliet and told her she was stretching the imagination of believability. "He's got to love dogs."

"Dogs?"

"Yep. I love dogs. I've always wanted one, but my parents never got one. I think my mom is allergic. He's got to be crazy about me. I don't want a cheater." She wrinkled her nose and finished off her pizza. "He has to not be a criminal, but I put it as *do the right thing* growing up. I just didn't realize I meant not be a criminal."

He chuckled. "You're not into bad boys."

She rolled her eyes. "The last two are to hold my hair back when I'm sick, and he's got to love to dance." She shrugged. "I was a kid. Don't judge but the fact my mom is even bringing that stuff up."

"Ten," he said.

"Huh?"

"You made a list of ten things you want your man to be," he said.

"I was a kid. It was some fun." She shrugged. "Juliet and Mackenzie made the same list. I'm sure a lot of kids do it. I mean, that time in their life is crazy. List making is the bomb, and it's ideal." She was done with the pizza. "With Mackenzie and Juliet coming, what are we going to do?"

"I don't know. How quick do you think it is to have a wedding?"

Eliza sighed. "Do you think we can pretend a company emergency?"

"My family would be pissed. I've done a couple

of them to get away from here early. They wanted me to settle down a few years ago, and a parade of single women were pretty much thrust in front of my nose."

She wasn't going to admit the thought of other women wanting him bothered her.

"What are we going to do?" Eliza asked.

"I have no idea."

This wasn't helping.

****

Juliet and Mackenzie made it the following morning. Eliza had been with them since and Preston, well, he was still reeling from the list of ten. That had to be the connection.

"I didn't think I'd find you out here," Roger said, coming toward the pool.

Preston lifted his whiskey glass. "Just out here relaxing."

"While they're all inside deciding how you're going to get married?"

"Yep."

"Okay, I need to know what you've done with my brother. He would never allow anyone to organize anything for him."

"I'm changing."

"Not that much."

Roger pushed his pants down, took off his shirt, and dived into the pool. "You know, when Trudy told me you were engaged, I thought it was a load of bullshit."

"You did?"

"Yeah. It's you. The only way to get engaged is for it to be some kind of elaborate event. You always went bigger than everyone else."

Preston laughed. "It's nothing personal that I do things bigger and better."

Roger snorted. "So with us finding out from our

sister, I figured you were doing some kind of thing to get her off your case, only it backfired."

"And now?" he asked.

"I've seen the way you are with Eliza, and you've never been like that with any other woman."

"How do you mean?"

Roger sighs. "I'm not a chick. I don't have to explain everything."

"Yeah, you do. I'm curious what you've seen." With the fact his parents were arranging a wedding for a fake engagement, and his carefully organized world was going down the crapper, he didn't see a problem in playing along.

"You notice her enter a room every single time. The way you watch her. She is all you can focus on. When she's not near you, you keep looking for her. It's like you're both connected with each other. She's the same, she'll watch you. There were a couple of times I wanted to tell you both to get a room. There's no faking that kind of shit."

"Nope, I wasn't faking." Preston finished his glass of whiskey. The burn was welcome.

He couldn't help but wonder if it would be so hard for him and Eliza to actually get married. They were not hurting anyone. They were great together.

The image of the broken condom flashed in his mind. There hadn't been any way to tell her about that.

He rubbed at his eyes.

Even though he didn't want to believe it, he knew a woman could get pregnant from that breakage.

"Are you okay?" Roger asked.

"Yeah, I'm fine. Do you know when Eliza is going to return?" Preston asked.

Just then, Juliet came running toward him. "Er, we kind of need you."

He climbed out of the pool and followed Juliet toward the front of the house.

Eliza was curled up in a ball on his parents' front lawn. The white summer dress she wore had ridden up her thighs.

Mackenzie sat with her.

"What's going on?" he asked.

"Er, a few too many tequila shots, and a whole load of confessions," Juliet said. "If her parents see her like this, they're going to be pissed. They didn't raise an alcoholic."

Eliza rolled over. "I'm not an alcoholic, but Preston is going to hate me when he has to marry me." She smiled up at him. "Aren't you, baby?"

He smiled.

A drunk Eliza was very cute. "Did someone have fun today?"

"I drank lots. Shh, don't tell my mommy. She will be so pissed." The last world was drawled out long.

He chuckled. "Come on, then, we better get you upstairs."

"He's good in bed," Eliza said, screaming out the words.

Juliet and Mackenzie sniggered.

"The list works. Preston," she said. "You are my ideal man. Will you marry me?" she asked.

He smirked. As he lifted her into his arms, she sighed and pressed her head against his chest. "You feel so warm and snuggly."

He loved the feel of her in his arms.

Carrying her across the field, he left Juliet and Mackenzie behind and carried her through the house to head upstairs.

At one point, she started singing a song he didn't recognize out of tune.

"I've been a bad girl," she said, covering her face.

He kicked their door closed and lowered Eliza to the bed.

"So you think I'm good in bed?" he asked.

"And a good kisser." She got to her feet and started to sway. "Do you dance?" She moved her hips left then right. "I love to dance. I want to dance."

Preston grabbed her hips when she seemed to sway a little too far left and right. He didn't want her falling to the floor. "I've got you."

"Are we going to get married?" she asked.

"I don't know."

"I never get drunk like this." She pressed her face against his chest.

Running his hands up and down her back, he tried to calm her. "It's okay. You're going to be okay." He kissed the top of her head.

"I'm going to be sick."

She ran away from him, and he caught up to her, immediately pulling her hair back so she wouldn't vomit on it.

Eliza threw up in the toilet. "Not good. So not good."

He rubbed her back and kept her hair out of the way.

"I've got you," he said.

"Why are you being so nice to me?" she asked. "I'm drunk at your parents'." She groaned. "I'm setting a bad example. They're going to hate me."

"No, my parents adore you."

"They adore our fakeness." She threw up some more, and he couldn't help but smile.

"It's okay. Get it all out."

"Wow, this is disgusting. Why do people get drunk again?" she asked.

"Because they enjoy the experience of getting drunk, just not all the aftermath. That part sucks."

She chuckled. "Sometimes you sound like a nerd."

"In case you didn't notice, I was one."

She snorted. "Yeah, and now look at you. You're the hot businessman all the women are fighting over."

"You think I'm hot?" he asked.

"Oh, please, you know I do. Ugh, this is so gross. You can never talk about this with anyone. I swear you to secrecy."

"What? About how you can't handle your liquor?" he asked, still rubbing her back.

She groaned again. "I'm barring myself from ever drinking again. That's it. I will never, ever, ever, ever, ever ... ugh, I think I'm going to be sick." She spewed up more.

He kept rubbing her back, trying to soothe her as she puked into the toilet. This was certainly a new experience for him.

"Never... drinking... again," she said. "It's the devil."

Preston stayed with her as she got herself together.

After going toward the bathtub, he started to fill it with water and bubbles for her to have a nice, long soak.

"What are you doing?" Eliza asked.

"You're going to take a bath, then I'm putting you to bed. At best tomorrow, you have a killer headache. At worst, you will still be throwing your guts up, and I'm not handling my parents, your parents, and your friends alone."

"Sissy," she said.

He chuckled, moving toward her. "You know, even looking disheveled and a little worse for wear, you're still fucking beautiful."

She tilted her head back and he saw the merest hint of a smile playing across her lips. "You think I'm beautiful?"

"I don't just think it. I know it." He helped her out of her clothes.

"I like that." She chuckled. "You think I'm beautiful."

"Is this going to go to your head?"

"Probably. What woman wouldn't let it go to her head?"

He couldn't help but smile as he stripped her of her clothes. He was only speaking the truth.

Helping Eliza into the tub, he heard her sigh.

"I rarely drink. I normally don't like it, but with everything going on, I felt I had to."

"You felt compelled to drink?" he asked.

"I don't know how we're going to get out of this mess," she said. "Do you have any ideas?"

He knelt by the edge of the bathtub. It was a shame he'd put bubbles into the water, covering her delectable body. All he wanted to do was take her back to his bedroom and kiss every single inch of her, but that time would come.

"Why don't we just let it play out?" he asked.

"You want to let our parents plan our wedding?"

"Would it be so bad?"

"Preston, clearly, you're drunk, and I'm the one who is still sober. Do you think it ends with them planning a wedding?" She shook her head. "No, it ends with them making us get married by the end of our vacation. That's what happens. There is a reason my parents are here, and my best friends." She sighed. "The only thing that is different is it won't be in December when the ground is covered in snow."

"It does look so beautiful covered in snow."

"I can't believe how similar our dream wedding is."

"I can't believe how sober you're sounding right now."

She laughed. "I'm not. I probably won't remember much of this conversation."

"You won't."

Eliza shook her head.

"Then how about I reveal this: I don't think it will be a bad thing, us getting married," he said.

She started to laugh. "I don't know when you turned into a jokester."

"I didn't."

"You want to get married?" she asked.

"I want a whole heap of things. Do you think it's just young girls who make a list of ten?"

There was a break of silence.

"I don't believe you."

"Believe me or not, it's true. We both had similar ideas, but mine were more directed to the goals in my life rather than anything else." He reached out and stroked some fingers through her hair.

"I like it when you do that," she said.

"Doing what?"

"Touching me. I shouldn't care, should I?"

"I like touching you." He pressed a kiss to her forehead. "Come on, let's get you washed and put to bed."

Eliza hadn't said no. She wasn't in a position to say yes.

He picked up the sponge and lathered it with soap, then began to clean her up. She spent a great deal of time groaning and cursing her body for not being able to move. He still found her cute.

With her body clean, he washed her hair, and then pulled the plug. She had no desire to throw up, so he grabbed a towel, wrapped it around her body, and carried her through to the main bedroom.

She did complain about him carrying her around, but like always, he ignored it and just did what he wanted to do. He put her in a pair of shorts and a tank top, helped her into bed, then crouched down, pushing some of her still damp hair off her face.

"I'm so tired," she said.

"Then sleep. I'll be back in a second with some food." He pressed a kiss to her temple.

"I hate food."

He smiled. That was the alcohol talking.

Preston left the bedroom and immediately went downstairs. He didn't like the thought of leaving her.

In a drunken state, anything could happen.

Juliet and Mackenzie were in the kitchen when he entered. They were clearly drinking coffee.

"How is she?" Juliet asked while Mackenzie stood.

"She's fine. Don't worry about it, I'm taking care of her. How did she get that bad?"

"We didn't realize how many shots she'd taken, as well as drinking a few shots of whiskey."

"It's fine. I can handle everything. She is being well taken care of."

The room was quiet as he got some bread and poured out a large pitcher of coffee. For himself, he actually made a sandwich, but for Eliza, dry bread was the key to soak up some of that alcohol.

"You're in love with her, aren't you?" Mackenzie asked.

He looked up, staring at Eliza's friend.

"I've got to get this to her. She needs to eat." And

he wasn't about to tell her best friends how he felt.

"She's in love with you too," Juliet said. "It's why she got so drunk."

"What? The thought of being in love with me was just too distasteful for her?" he asked.

"No, it was the knowledge that she had fallen in love with you long before coming here. Part of her wishes she could marry you right here," Juliet said. "But to her, this is all fake, remember? Not a single part of this is real."

It had started out like that, but it wasn't what he felt anymore, and he couldn't help but wonder if Eliza felt the same way.

Chapter Sixteen

Getting drunk was completely irresponsible.

Eliza vowed to never do it again.

Preston had seen her at one of her worst moments. She rarely ever got drunk. That one time at work when he announced they were engaged to his sister was the only time she'd done it in so long.

She was the responsible one.

The down-to-earth one.

Yet, the last few days, it felt like her life was running away from her and there wasn't a single thing she could do about it.

Running fingers through her hair, she tried to think of something, anything that would help her understand why she had vomited so bad.

Preston was nowhere to be found.

Juliet and Mackenzie had left her a note, saying they would be back, but they were going to visit the diner. They were going to see Melinda. They were both fascinated with the woman who foretold life stories.

Walking through the house, she was surprised by how empty it felt. She went to the kitchen to grab a large mug of coffee. It was still so warm, and rather than stay in the kitchen, she took herself outside, where she found her mother and Marsha organizing the wedding.

They had several catalogs and magazines all open. Notebooks were in their hands, and they were laughing about something.

Eliza wanted to make her escape undetected, but her mother chose that moment to glance up.

"Eliza, honey, we've been waiting for you to get up. Preston told us you weren't feeling well."

"I wasn't. Do you know where he is?" She had no other excuse she could think of. There was no quick resolve for her to make a quick escape. She was at their parents' mercy.

Had Preston done this on purpose?

She showed no weakness as she moved toward them and took a seat. "What is all of this?"

Her mother looked so proud. "This, sweetheart, is the wedding you always wanted."

"I have not had this much fun in so long," Marsha said. "I had no idea you and Preston had such similar ideas. You both love roses, did you know that?"

Eliza smiled. She didn't know that. When he'd broken up with women in the past, he often ordered them tulips, never roses. Why?

She made a note to ask him. Not that it was important, and it was only a minor detail.

"Don't you think you should be planning your anniversary?" Eliza asked. "Preston and I can handle this."

"This is no trouble. In fact, it has given me a sense of direction. For instance, Roger, Kian, and Andrew have gone with their wives to go and test the cake, which is a relief. They were getting a little underfoot," Marsha said.

"We have already gotten the wedding dress altered to your measurements, and Trudy took care of the fine details." Her mother got to her feet and opened a box.

Eliza felt close to losing it.

This wasn't what she had hoped to achieve when talking to her parents.

She was just about to open her mouth to tell them to stop when her mother held up the most beautiful white wedding dress she'd ever seen. Back in the day, the plunging v-neck and exposed arms had seemed risqué at the time, but she remembered people back home who had been at the wedding who only said nice things about her mother and just how beautiful she looked.

"It looks amazing," she said.

"I want you to try it on."

"Isn't that bad luck?" Eliza asked.

There was no way she should try it on. No way at all, but within minutes, she stood in the main living room, in a wedding dress that fit her like a second skin. It was so beautiful. Running her hands over her waist, she turned this way and that and smiled. "It is … amazing."

"I must commend Trudy. She did an amazing job," Marsha said.

"Oh, honey, I think I'm going to cry."

"Please, Mom, don't cry. If you cry, then I cry, and we all cry." She felt tears well in her eyes. This wasn't the time to be crying.

Her mother waved her hands in front of her face. "No. I can contain myself, but to see my only child like this. It's a dream come true."

Someone cleared their throat, and Eliza looked up in time to see Preston had stepped into the room.

No one spoke.

No one moved.

And then, chaos ensued.

Her mother and Marsha fussed him out of the room, and Eliza began to wriggle out of the dress.

This was playing along in the pretend.

She and Preston were not getting married.

Her mother came back toward her as Marsha went to deal with Preston.

"Did you see his face?" she asked.

"No."

"He is so besotted with you. Your father will be pleased. You know he's going to do his routine."

Eliza groaned. "No. No. No. I ban Father from

giving my boss the gun routine. It's not good. No, scrap that, it is never good when he does it. He's not supposed to threaten my boss with impending death."

"I think it is already done, honey." Her mother kissed her head, helping her out of the dress.

She wanted to get dressed back into it, but instead, she slid into the dress she'd put on. With the headache she had, there was no place for her to try and wriggle into any item of clothing. The dress went right over her head with ease.

"Are you okay?" her mother asked.

"Yeah, yeah, I'm fine. I'm going to go and see how Preston is doing." She went to leave, but her mother caught her face and pressed a kiss to her cheek. "What was that for?"

"I can't just kiss my daughter because I love her?"

She smiled but knew her mother was just happy to be organizing a wedding. Eliza found Marsha in the kitchen.

"Preston has gone to the pool," Marsha said.

"Thank you."

She went toward the door leading out to the garden, but Marsha stopped her, placing a swimsuit into her hands. "Just in case." She pointed toward the pantry with a brow raised.

Eliza snuck into the pantry and slid into the swimsuit. Her hair wasn't pinned up.

Sliding the dress back into place, she left the pantry. Marsha was nowhere to be found.

The moment she was in the garden, she took a deep breath and followed the path down to the pool.

She waited as Preston finished swimming a lap.

"Sorry you had to see that," she said.

"I wasn't."

She crouched down so she was a little closer to him. "You're not sorry that your fake fiancée was trying on a wedding dress?"

"Nope. Can I tell you how beautiful you looked?" he asked.

"You can only say that if you think it is true."

"Then my statement stands. You looked beautiful."

Her heart raced. "You think I'm beautiful."

"We had this conversation last night, but I see the tequila wiped your memory, which sucks for me. I think you're an incredibly beautiful woman, Eliza."

"You're not just saying that."

"I've got no reason to just say it. Do you care to join me?" he asked.

The water did look so inviting.

Getting to her feet, she pulled the dress over her head and tossed it toward the nearest lounge chair, where Preston's clothes were also abandoned.

She moved toward the stairs, and Preston was already there, putting his hands on her waist and helping her into the water.

"I'm quite capable, you know," she said.

He spun her around and pressed her up against the side of the pool. "I have no doubt you're more than capable." He was so close to her. When he nudged her up against the counter, she gasped as she felt the hard length of his cock against her stomach. "But I wanted an excuse to touch you. Is that such a crime?"

"Preston, don't you think this is getting out of hand?" she asked.

She couldn't help but close her eyes as his fingers skimmed up the sides of her body, his touch so close to her breasts, but never getting there. Sinking her teeth into her lip, she waited, but he pulled back.

"No, do you?"

Opening her eyes, she saw he'd given her some space.

"They're planning our wedding."

"I know."

Was she talking to a brick wall?

She clicked her fingers. "Marriage. The ring. All of it, Preston. This isn't a game."

"I know."

She jerked back a few feet. "You don't care?"

"Why would I care?" he asked. "My parents approve of you. They've gotten your parents to help. Your friends are here. What are you so afraid of?"

"This is a lie."

"Is it?" he asked, cupping her face. "When I touch you, does it feel like a lie?"

"You're talking about sex. Marriage is in the long term."

"I haven't seen my parents so freaking happy like this for me."

She covered his hands with her own. "Because they believe we're really engaged."

"Why don't we be?" he asked.

This made Eliza pause. "What?"

"I think it's time for us to make a new deal."

"You know what, I cannot talk to you right now." Eliza padded toward the end of the pool and climbed out.

She didn't want to go back to the main house as there was just too much going on.

Ignoring her dress, she went toward the back of the house, passing several rose beds as she did.

Eliza didn't get far before he'd caught up with her.

"Wait," he said.

She was just about to pass the pool house when

he captured her wrist. Eliza didn't fight him as he opened the door and pressed her up against the wall.

"The only thing that makes sense to me right now is this," he said, slamming his lips down on hers.

She pressed her hands to his chest, intent on pushing him away, but with the feel of mouth and his body against hers on her, she couldn't do it.

The hands that were supposed to push him away gripped him even tighter. Sliding them around his back, up toward his neck, she didn't break the kiss either. Instead, she kissed him back with the hunger she felt.

This was getting so hard for her because she already accepted that she'd fallen in love with this man. Preston Boone had gotten underneath her skin, and there was no getting away from it.

He tugged the strap down her body, and she didn't put up a fight, more than happy to let it fall away.

Within seconds, her swimsuit and his trunks were on the floor. He had her hiked up against the wall, and his hard cock slid inside her.

They didn't stop kissing.

He felt incredible.

This made sense.

This was easy.

Sex was always easy.

Preston moved them away from the wall and took them toward the sofa. Collapsing against it, she stared down at where they were connected. He licked his thumb and stroked it across her clit.

She cried out, moaning his name as he worked her toward an orgasm that had her curling her toes.

"Fuck, you look so beautiful like that."

He grabbed her hips and began to pound inside her. The sounds of their bodies slapping together, their moans, it all echoed around the room. Their needs so animalistic, so primal. Their hunger knew no bounds, and when she felt the kick of Preston's cock inside her as he came, she knew no matter what, they had changed the course of their lives forever.

****

Preston hadn't used a condom.

It hadn't been his intention to get her into the pool house and take her without one, but that was exactly what happened, and he couldn't complain. The feel of her tight cunt wrapped around his length was sheer heaven.

He'd never taken anyone without a condom before. Eliza was his first and only woman.

Seeing her in that wedding dress, something had hit him. Along with her best friends' words, he wasn't afraid of the future. He knew Eliza was it for him. However, she was fighting this between them.

After their impromptu sex in the pool house, she avoided him again, and that drove him crazy. Either she avoided him or his family was working double time to take her away from him.

He didn't like the idea of either, so he was going with her just plain avoiding him.

Rubbing at his temples, he glanced over the file.

Standing in the house he'd already put his signature on and was just waiting for the final details to come through, he glanced through the Aguire file.

He'd called Eliza multiple times to remind her to be here.

The house seemed to mock him as Eliza ignored him, and this was his dream house.

He wanted to talk to his father about everything that he was going through, but to do that would be to admit he'd fucked up, and that wasn't going to happen. The last thing he wanted to do was to have his father glare at him with disapproval.

Preston couldn't believe the amount of detail Eliza obtained on Aguire. The man was all about family, loyalty, and community. It said it right there in the pages.

At the sound of his door opening, he closed the file and turned to see Eliza, dressed in a pair of shorts, flip-flops, and a crop top, entering the house. He also hadn't gone for a business suit, but instead wore khaki shorts and a shirt.

The weather was hot as fuck outside.

"You came," he said.

She gasped and whirled around. "Preston, where is Mr. Aguire?"

"Not here, but we've got ten minutes. He'll be on time. I've got no doubt."

"I thought we were going to meet at a hotel?" she asked. "That was what I organized."

Preston shrugged. "He called me this morning while you had disappeared. Told me that he was interested in meeting me soon, and I let him know I had purchased a place here and was going to do some measurements and prepare to furnish it."

"So this part is all real?" Eliza asked. "You're going to stay here?"

"I'm going to come back home, I think." This house wasn't just for him though. "Eliza, we've got to talk."

She shook her head. "No, we don't need to talk about anything."

"Did you take the morning-after pill?"

"No, I haven't taken it. I haven't had time to get to the pharmacy for it."

"Then don't take it," he said.

"Preston, we had unprotected sex."

"And I'm clean, and I know you are as well."

"Oh, really?" she asked, then immediately frowned. "Scrap whatever I just said. I'm not thinking straight right now. Look, I don't know what's happening."

"Marry me," he said.

"What?"

He blew out a breath. "You heard me. Marry me?"

"I can't believe this. You want me to marry you even though this is all a lie. You'd go that far not to tell your parents the truth, or is this about Aguire?" she asked.

"This has nothing to do with him."

"You know he'd like you more being a family man. Was yesterday a spur-of-the-moment thing?" she asked.

"You know damn well it was," he said. "I did not plan what happened yesterday."

"So you just happened to drag me into the pool house conveniently without a condom?" she asked.

"Damn it, Eliza. I know you think I'm great and powerful and wonderful, but even my skill has limits. I didn't make you go that way, did I? The only reason we were near the pool house was because that was the direction you took. Not me. I was following you. If you'd gone back to the house, we would've gone to my bedroom, where there are plenty of condoms," he said. "You also didn't push me away."

"Oh, right, so it is all my fault now, is it? Is that what you're saying?"

"Damn it, Eliza, I'm saying I can't get enough of you. The moment I'm near you, I can't think. I've never felt this way about a woman before, and you're driving me crazy only seeing the bad things." He growled. He wanted to say more, but the doorbell rang. "Fuck!"

Eliza glanced behind her. "Look, I'm sorry. I know how important this deal is for you. We won't argue while he's here."

"I don't want to argue with you when he's gone."

"Preston, I don't know what you want from me."

He was going to tell her straight, but of course, the bell rang again. It was getting in the damn way.

Eliza moved toward the door, and he followed her, putting a hand on the base of her back. He forced a smile to his lips when he caught sight of Aguire.

"Mr. Aguire," Eliza said. "Pleasure as always."

"This place is really something. You only just snapped this place up?" he asked.

"Yeah, my sister-in-law told me all about it, and what can I say, I love it, and so does Eliza." He put his hands on her shoulders.

Having Aguire here wasn't what he wanted. Being back in Westcliffe Heights had started to change his priorities.

"This place is amazing. I am surprised, Mr. Boone," he said.

"What is there to be surprised about?" Preston asked.

"I never pegged you as a small-town guy."

"Born and raised here. This is my hometown."

"I get that with all the Boone properties. You've got it made here, son. What made you leave and go to the city?"

He rubbed Eliza's shoulders. "Since I was a kid, I had this need to know I could make it on my own. It wasn't that I wasn't grateful for all that my parents did, I was. I love them for the life they've given me, but they have also told me what is important in life. It took me some time and lost direction, but I now know what I want out of life. More than I've ever known."

Aguire nodded. "That, I can understand. The path to success is often a rocky road with misdirected priorities. I respect that. I had the same epiphany myself. It can be a lonely road. May I have a tour?"

"Of course," Preston said.

He took Eliza's hand, and rather than talk business, he took Aguire on the tour. When he didn't have a clue what to do with the room, he let Eliza take over, directing her own thoughts and feelings on how to decorate the house.

Before too long, two hours had gone, and they stood in the garden.

Aguire smiled. "When I was told that you were engaged to your assistant, I thought it was a load of bullshit to get me to agree to my land. Seeing the two of you, I know the truth. There is real love there, and I can put my faith in a man who is willing to take a leap like that." Aguire held out his hand. "We can sit down and talk about the fine details, but the land you want is yours. I have faith in what you do."

Preston shook the man's hand.

"I better be getting back," Aguire said.

They moved through the house and let Aguire out the front door. Preston gave him a final wave as he got to his car at the gate.

Stepping back into the house, he took a deep breath.

"You got it," Eliza said.

She moved toward the door, but he grabbed her arm. "Eliza, don't go."

"Preston, this wasn't supposed to happen. The plan was to tell a little lie to your parents. It has gotten more elaborate, and right now, I cannot deal with just how … far everything is going. I need to take a walk. To clear my head."

There was so much he wanted to say to get her to stay so they could talk, but it remained lodged in his throat.

The house fucking mocked him with its silence. Back in the city, he'd often closed his office door just to enjoy the silence so he could think. Now he wanted Eliza, he'd take Aguire if he could just to have a conversation.

Instead, he left his home, locking the door behind him, and began to walk back to the house.

It was dark. He didn't know when night had fallen, but as he entered his home, his father came out of his office.

"Ah, Preston, you're back."

"Have you seen Eliza?" he asked.

"She is out with the ladies. Your mother decided she needed a girls' night on the town. She got all the women together, and Eliza didn't even have time to breathe before she was swept up in it all. You know how your mother is."

He laughed. "Yep, once she gets an idea of something, that is it. You either go along for the ride or get out of the way." He smiled just thinking about it. His mother was a force to be reckoned with.

"Come and have a drink with me," Greg said.

Preston walked into his father's office and collapsed down into the chair.

"Rough day?"

"You could say that."

"Do you want to tell me about it?" Greg asked, pouring out a glass of whiskey.

There was no way he could tell his father anything.

"Eliza and I had a ... disagreement is all," he said.

"Ah, to be young, in love, and at each other's throats."

"You make that sound like a good thing. Isn't that a bad thing?"

"Depends on how you view it. Your mother and I always had our disagreements, but nothing ever got in the way of our love for each other." Greg smiled. "I'm not going to get into the details."

"Please, don't. There is only so much I can handle about my parents. I accepted you had sex enough times to create your kids, but that is it."

"Just think, when you have children of your own someday, you get to be the gross one."

Preston lifted his glass, but he didn't take a snip. "Dad, how did you convince Mom you were in love with her?"

"There was no need to convince her. She knew every single day of her life since we were ten. Told her every single day."

"And to tell her you loved her wasn't hard?"

Greg squinted and pursed his lips. "What are you trying to ask me, son? Have you never told Eliza that you love her?"

"Of course I have." The lie was easy, but the feeling afterward wasn't something he liked at all. "I haven't told her in a little while."

"Then, son, you need to change that. The key to a happy marriage is to swallow your pride and admit you're wrong. To listen. To be there for her. You have got to go and tell your girl right this second that she is yours, and have no doubt about it."

Preston didn't get off his ass. He stared into his glass, thinking it was figuratively speaking.

The whiskey was taken from him, and within seconds, he was nudged out of the door.

Chapter Seventeen

"Okay, you're surrounded by amazing music, good food and beer, amazing company, and you look like someone has just told you your imaginary dog has died," Mackenzie said.

"What gives?" Juliet asked.

Eliza looked up from her beer.

The other women were on the dance floor, dancing it up. She wanted to be on the dance floor. Instead, she was staring at her beer and thinking about Preston.

"It's nothing. Go on. Go and dance."

Her friends each shared a look and Eliza sighed.

"It's nothing, okay? I am fine. There's nothing for you to worry about. Go and have some fun. Dance it up. Please. I will join you when I can."

"Nope," Juliet said.

"Not happening," Mackenzie said.

"We're here until you can come and dance. Not a moment later," Juliet said, tipping the bottle against her lips. "This place is solid though."

Eliza smiled.

"Tell us what's going on," Mackenzie said. "You wouldn't talk to us this morning."

"And you have been deep in avoiding," Juliet said. "We can't help you unless you tell us everything."

She took a deep breath. "It's not anything bad. At least, I don't think it is entirely bad, but I don't know. I'm not exactly the best judge of character when it comes to Preston."

"So your boss is the one who is making you sad?" Mackenzie asked.

"It's not him. Have you seen our mothers? They're organizing a wedding. You guys are here, and you know I love you both, but you know what it means." She sighed and dropped her head to the table. "Ugh, it feels sticky." She sat up and grabbed a napkin, rubbing at her temple. "I'm not drinking another thing. I refuse to."

"I'll go and order you a soda," Mackenzie said, already slipping off her stool and heading to the bar.

"Do you think you should come clean?" Juliet asked.

"I don't know. Preston ... he wants to get married."

"He does?"

"I don't know if I can do that. Live the lie."

"Look, babe, I love you, but sometimes you don't see everything going on around you. Have you ever considered that maybe it's not a lie?" Juliet asked.

"What do you mean?"

"Have you ever thought that maybe Preston wants to marry you?"

She shook her head. "No. He doesn't want to marry me. He can have any woman he wants."

"Yeah, and you're the woman he seeks out. You're the woman I've seen him watching the few times I've met him."

"It's not like that. I work for him."

"Babe, I work for men, okay? Believe me, they only stare at a woman like that if they want her."

Eliza's face heated when she thought about Preston. The way he touched her. The fire he built inside her.

Juliet finished her drink as Mackenzie arrived back at the table.

"I need to pee," Juliet said.

"Me too. Do you?" Mackenzie asked.

"Nah, I'm good. You two go."

Her friends left her alone, and she stared at her

soda. She had no desire to drink.

Laughter pulled her attention, and she looked toward the dance floor. Her mother was having a great time. All of the women were. On the way over, Lydia had told her girls' night happened every so often as Marsha liked to get away from it all from time to time.

"You shouldn't be alone in this bar," Preston said.

She'd been so busy looking at his mother and hers, she hadn't seen him enter. "Preston, what are you doing here?"

"I heard my woman went out for ladies' night, and coming to this bar, I knew way too many men would be wanting to score with her. I don't like seeing you look lonely."

"No one has asked me to dance, and my friends went to the bathroom. I'm not that big of a catch, Preston."

He held out his hand.

She wanted to deny him, but she saw no reason to cause a scene. It was bad enough arguing with him and then having to act all loved up with Aguire looking on. She was exhausted.

Sliding her hand into his, she followed him onto the dance floor.

Regardless of the song being upbeat, Preston pulled her into his arms and danced as if it was a slow song.

"What's going on, Preston?"

"Nothing. We're going to dance."

At first, she was tense in his arms. The song wasn't designed to be danced with slowly. Her heart raced as his fingers traced across her back.

She loved his touch, craved it. Closing her eyes, she rested her head against his chest.

"Feel, Eliza."

She did feel, and that was the problem. This wasn't just an agreement anymore. They were not just bargaining for stupid stuff. She didn't care about her job. No, this was a matter of the heart, and it meant far more to her than some job.

Slowly, she relaxed against him, and the moment she did, Preston took over. He grabbed her hands and began to dance with her.

He swung his hips, and she stared at him at first, wondering what he was doing.

"Come on, baby, dance."

"What are you doing?" she asked, laughing.

"Showing you a side to me that no one gets to see unless they're too far drunk to remember."

He let go of one hand and started to shake it in beat to the music.

Preston Boone was a terrible dancer, but she also saw with the smile on his lips that he was having the time of his life. He wanted to dance, and his laughter was just infectious.

Joining in, Eliza showed him why she only danced in her apartment, rarely in front of everyone.

They spun away from each other, and backed to butts, rubbed up and down, twirling.

Preston pulled her in close and dropped her back. She let out a little squeal. "Please, don't drop me. Please."

"Never. Haven't I shown you clear enough that I will always catch you, Eliza?"

The song changed, but he didn't let her go. His grip was firm. Strong. There was no sign of weakness.

The way he looked at her, it was like he … no, she couldn't believe it. He wasn't in love with her, was he?

Everything she thought she knew, it was like it wasn't real.

Preston lifted her up.

This time, the song had changed to a slow one, and she moved into his arms, closing her eyes. In his arms, she felt safe, comfortable, whole. She knew she was in love with him, but her feelings for him hadn't started since coming to Westcliffe Heights. They started before that. She couldn't even put a time stamp on how he made her feel.

Pulling away from him, she shook her head. "I can't do this."

There was no way she could pretend to be in love with him. Not anymore. She wasn't hiding from her feelings.

He didn't stop her as she turned on her heel.

Juliet and Mackenzie looked worried about her, but she told them not to. She was heading home.

Leaving the bar, she took a deep breath of air, tears filling her eyes.

"Eliza, don't go," Preston said.

She spun around to see Preston, her mother, his mother, and his sisters-in-law all leaving the bar. There was no way she could cause a scene and bear to let them know this was all lies.

Forcing a smile to her lips, she moved close to him. When she was near him, he wrapped his arm around her shoulders. "I've got you."

"Eliza, is everything okay?" her mother asked.

"Yeah, it's fine." She hated lying. She'd never been the kind of person to lie to her mother.

"Well, seeing as Lydia is the designated driver for tonight," Marsha said. "And you don't seem to have drunk a wink, I will let you take Eliza home."

"I was already going to, Mom," Preston said.

His mother gave his cheek an affectionate tap. "Good boy."

She wanted to argue with Marsha, but again, the whole scene would have been too much.

Her mother pulled her in for a hug. "Love you, honey. See you back at the house."

Eliza nodded.

Preston walked her toward his car and held open the passenger seat. She didn't argue with him and slid into the seat, waiting.

The door closed, and she couldn't help but flinch.

He climbed behind the wheel and started up the car.

For several minutes, they drove in silence, and it wasn't long before they were entering his street.

She rubbed at her temples, feeling the start of a headache.

"I can't keep lying like this," she said.

He pulled up onto the drive. "I know that."

"So, tomorrow, I will be handing in my resignation and I will also be leaving, after breakfast." She hadn't made any plans like this. Just the thought of never seeing Preston again, she felt like her whole world was falling apart. She swiped at her tears. They were useless.

"Eliza," he said.

She held her hand up. "I'm going to go in first." She unbuckled her seatbelt and rushed toward the front of the house.

Greg was at the door, along with his sons.

"Are you okay?" he asked.

"Yes, I am. Thank you so much. I had a wonderful time tonight, but I think I must have eaten something. I'm feeling a little sick." She made her excuses quickly.

She went straight to Preston's room. She didn't shut the door and went to the bathroom.

Stripping out of her clothes, she stepped into the shower and turned on the spray. The cold water covered her body in tiny little ice droplets that didn't stop. She released a cry and tilted her head back.

This is for the better.

There is no way you can continue working for him with the way you feel.

The lies kept forming in her head.

Each one seeming to be worse than the last.

The truth was that after working with Preston, she'd fallen in love with him, and rather than turn her back and do the healthy thing, she'd stayed.

The tears fell thick and fast.

Covering her face, she gave way to the sobbing. The past few weeks, playing his fake fiancée, had been the best of her life. She'd enjoyed every single touch, caress, and just being near him.

His family was amazing.

This town was exciting.

Melinda's premonition had been terrifying, but she'd loved it. There was not a part of her time here she hadn't enjoyed. Going to his den, making love, fucking, just being with him. She had loved every single second, and to get to see a part of the man he never showed the world, that had been even better.

The shower heated up quickly, and she turned it off, wrapping a towel around her. She used another towel on her body.

After drying off, she changed into a pair of sleep shorts and one of Preston's shirts, which still smelled like him. The scent of him wrapped around her, comforted her.

Entering the bedroom, dressed and dried, she

looked at him.

He sat on the bed.

"I'll be out in a minute."

She nodded and went straight to the bed. Climbing beneath the covers, she lay down and watched the door.

There was no sign of him.

She heard the shower as it turned on, and after several minutes, it turned off, signaling the end of the shower.

He didn't make her wait for long, entering the bedroom, dressed in a pair of boxer briefs.

She closed her eyes but sensed him as he moved, going from the shower to his side of the bed. The bed moved as he slid inside.

She waited.

She hadn't put a valley of pillows down.

More than anything, she wanted him to hold her, but he didn't reach for her. Not for a few seconds.

Tears leaked out of her eyes, and when she thought it was pointless to give up hope, one of his hands banded around her waist, pulled her close, and his lips pressed against her neck.

Now, this felt complete.

****

Preston couldn't let her go without her knowing the truth. That was his first thought the next morning. The next was that he didn't want to go back to the city. Westcliffe Heights was his home. Being back here for longer than a few days had helped him to realize what he'd been missing out on.

Being his own boss, he had all the capabilities to make this work. To finally come back home, but what he didn't have was Eliza.

Waking up with her in his arms, going to sleep

with her in them, laughing, joking, sharing those rare moments that couples do. He wanted it all.

The only way to get it all was to make his move.

By the time he finished with his morning shower, Eliza had left the bedroom. Her bags were packed and laid on the bed.

Preston stared at them, knowing in his heart that he didn't want her to go.

He got changed and went to the back of his closet, where he had kept some little items and tokens from the years when he was a kid. There were a few poems. A necklace Trudy had made for him when she was a little kid, and neatly folded, slid between the pages in a copy of his favorite book, was his list.

Not opening it, he slid it into his back pocket, returned his box to his closet, and walked down toward the breakfast table.

As usual, everyone was already downstairs. The heavy scent of his mother's cooking filled the air.

Juliet and Mackenzie sat on either side of Eliza, and his woman looked pale. He didn't like that.

Taking a seat opposite her, he stared at her, but she wouldn't meet his gaze.

"Ah, Preston, so pleased you could join us," Marsha said.

"How can you run a company if you sleep in, big bro?" Roger asked.

He smiled, but it didn't quite reach his eyes. "This is my rest time. I've had no reason to relax."

Staring at Eliza, he wanted her to look at him. To give him a single indication that she loved him. He knew what her friends had told him, but she'd never said the words to him.

"We have been looking at venues, Preston," Eliza's mother said. "For your wedding."

Marsha chuckled. "How do you feel about getting married at two different places, and then coming back here?"

With each word spoken, even in jest, Eliza tensed up. This was no longer fun. It was no longer a game.

"Eliza and I are not getting married," Preston said.

This time, she looked at him, and he stared right back at her.

The table had gone silent.

"Eliza has never been my fiancée. I told Trudy that to get her off my case and for you to not go out of your way and get a whole load of women lined up for me to date." He stood up. "Eliza and I made an agreement. She would get to keep her job so long as she played the role of my fiancée. We had ground rules for limited kissing, touching, and pretty much every single scenario you could think of. It's what makes her the best PA I've ever had, and one of the many reasons I'm in love with her."

"What are you doing?" she asked.

"I'm telling the truth. I will not allow this to continue, not like this." He pulled out his list. "You made a list of the top ten attributes you wanted in your man. I didn't make the same list, but I made a list of everything I wanted out of life." He started to open the folded piece of paper to read out loud.

"Just wait a minute, you and Eliza are not engaged?" Roger asked.

"No."

"What has this been about?" Kian asked.

"I've been falling in love with her," Preston said. "That's no lie."

"Preston," Eliza said.

"Hear me out. I have told the truth in front of our

families, and they know that we're not together, but I am now declaring in front of them, Eliza Drake, that I am completely in love with you, and I want to spend the rest of my life with you." He glanced down at his list. "I wanted to be my own boss by starting my own company. I did that. I want to find a nice house in the country to call my own." He turned toward Lydia. "I still want my house." He looked toward Eliza. "And I want to share it with you." He licked his lips. "I wanted to own a dog, then a cat. I don't know why I want to own a cat, they're disgusting, but I want both. A dog and a cat. I want to have a load of kids. The more the better. I didn't hate being an older brother. I haven't been the best son or brother the past few years, but I wouldn't trade this family for anything."

Tears were in her eyes, but he looked down and continued.

"I want to get married. Fall in love. Live my happy ever after. I want to be a good husband, and above all else, I wanted to be an amazing father." He looked toward his dad. "You taught me how to be a good man."

Then he turned back to her. "I'm in love with you, Eliza. I want to share my life with you. I'm not lying. I'm not acting. I'm telling you the truth, and you're probably going to hate this, but the condom broke."

There was a gasp.

"I want us to be together forever," he said. "Melinda told me I would find my woman of ten. I had no idea what she meant, but now I do." He held his list up. "At first I thought it was your list. The top ten of everything you wanted out of man, but it's not. It's my list. It's the woman I think about when I read my list, and when I think about my life, it's all you. I am in love with you."

He rounded the table and went to her side, sinking to his knee in front of her.

"This is my heart, Eliza. This is me. There is no one I want more. Will you be my wife?" he asked.

"I can't believe you're doing this," Eliza said.

"I can't let you walk away. I don't want to live my life without you in it. The past three years have been incredible and not because of work, but because every single day I walked into my building looking forward to seeing you. That was all I wanted. Every day. To see your face." He took her hand. "Do you love me?"

The seconds it took for her to answer were the worst of his life.

"More than anything."

He got to his feet, cupped her face, and kissed her. Sinking his fingers into her hair, he kissed her harder than he ever had.

Eliza moaned.

"Okay, am I the only one who is a little pissed that he lied?" Kian asked.

"Get over it, son," Marsha said. "His heart was in the right place."

He broke the kiss. "Marry me," he said.

"Yes."

"Have my kids?"

"Yes. Everything, yes, I want to marry you. I'm in love with you."

"Do you have a new ring, son?" Greg asked.

Preston glanced back at his dad and shook his head. "No, the ring I picked out was chosen from the heart. I didn't give her a substandard ring. I gave her the one I knew I wanted her to keep. You're my life, Eliza Drake, and I'm so sorry I waited three years to make you mine."

She put her hand to his chest. "Am I awake?"

"Yes, but if we're not, then I never want to wake up." Ignoring their parents, he kissed her again.

He took the leap, and now, Eliza was his and he was never going to give her back.

Eliza pulled away and smiled. "You owe Adam and Natasha a hundred dollars."

Preston burst out laughing. He'd forgotten all about that bet with his friends, but he had told Eliza about it late one night. That was the last he had thought of it. They were going to get a kick out of this. He hadn't told them anything since he got here. "Technically, I only owe Natasha," he said. "And I want to say, it is the best hundred bucks I've ever spent."

"I love you."

Epilogue

Five years later

"That was Juliet. She'll be here in an hour," Eliza said.

She put the phone into the cradle and walked into the sitting room. They had finished putting the decorations on the tree an hour ago, but her husband sat on the floor, a baby in his arms, while also putting the finishing pieces to the puzzle for Brendan.

Eliza smiled down at her little family.

"Mackenzie already texted. She's at my folks' place."

It wasn't Christmas without her friends and their whole family together. Her parents often came to Westcliffe Heights to be with Greg and Marsha. It was a friendship that had started five years ago, and it had grown from strength to strength.

She moved toward her husband's side, sitting next to him as Brendan clapped his hands.

"I did it, Daddy, I did it."

"You sure did, son. Do you want to head upstairs, get changed? Mom promised milk and cookies."

"Warm milk?" Brendan asked.

"Since when did I do anything but?" Eliza asked.

He gave the air a fist pump.

She smiled.

He was five years old, a bubble of fun, and so tiring at times. After Preston's proposal, they had gotten married the day after his parents' anniversary. Three months after that, she found out she was pregnant.

Preston had made it his mission to bring their lives to Westcliffe, and she was so pleased he had because being pregnant and surrounded by family had been a true gift. Her best friends still had their lives back in the city, and until they settled down, they had come to Westcliffe Heights. Now, they alternated between holidays going to each other's prospective houses, enjoying the life they always wanted.

Laura gurgled in Preston's arms.

"Fuck me, Eliza, I never knew I could be this happy," he said.

"Ah, language." She wrinkled her nose. "We don't want our babies to pick up bad habits."

"They will never hear me say anything but good words." He gripped the back of her neck, tilting her head back, and even after five years, his touch sent a spiral of need racing through her body. "And tonight, I'm going to worship your body."

She laughed. "I gave birth three weeks ago."

"I know, so when Brendan and Laura are down for the night, I'm going to draw you a bath, wash every single inch of your body, and then I'm going to give you a massage, and feed you chocolate ice cream. Does that sound like the kind of worship you want?"

"It's a start." She cupped his cheek, staring into his eyes. "I love you."

"And I am in love with you."

He kissed her again, and Eliza knew her life, no matter what chaos they faced, was complete.

The End

www.samcrescent.com

EVERNIGHT PUBLISHING ®

www.evernightpublishing.com